I0691906

THE COUNCIL

~ * ~

BOOK 3
THE VAMPIRE CHRONICLES
OF JACK HOLLADAY

BY

STEVE KREBS

Autumn Twilight Publishing
Pueblo***Colorado

The Council © 2014 All rights reserved by Steve Krebs

Autumn Twilight Publishing, LLC

For information:
Autumn Twilight Publishing, LLC
2209 E Evans Ave
Pueblo, Colorado 81004

http://crimson-nights.wix.com/vampire-chronicles

ISBN: 978-0-615-95097-6

Book Cover designed by Steve Krebs

Printed in the United States of America

Dedication

I would like to wish a special thanks to the following people for their help:

- }   My mom for telling me, "Never give up."
- }   Dennis Wiseman for being a great fan and friend.
- }   Ron Diller for sticking with me from the very beginning and giving me ideas for the cover.

My biggest thanks is to my wife and kids for being patient with me and encouraging.

My final thanks goes out to everyone who reads this book and who has followed along since the beginning. I really hope you like this novel as much as the last two.

The Council is the third book in The Vampire Chronicles of Jack Holladay series. Also look for Crimson Nights ISBN # 978-0-578-04920-5 and Silver Moon ISBN # 978-0-6155172-8-5. These books can be found at http://crimson-nights.wix.com/vampire-chronicles and other book stores.

Thanks
Steve Krebs

Chapter One

The name is Jack Holladay and I'm, once again, a pizza delivery driver. I'm also an informant for the F.B.I.P.A., which stands for the Federal Bureau of Investigations of Paranormal Activity. They are a special department of the F.B.I. which deals with the supernatural. The majority of the populace doesn't believe in monsters and they want to keep it that way. If the word would get out that the things in the night that goes bump really does exist, there would be mass panic. Then who knows, maybe the Salem witch trials would start up all over again.

Now that Katrina has been taken into custody by Agent Jacopo, things have been quiet. Well, for me and Selene anyway. It's been a little over a month since the werewolf war and we still haven't heard anything from the Vampire Council.

Jean Luke established himself as the new master vampire of the city. Tyrone didn't like the idea of letting Katrina being taken, but what choice did he have. If he interfered Agent Jacopo would have just had Tyrone staked. He was just looking for a reason to kill all the vampires anyway.

The only thing keeping them alive was me, in more ways than one. Agent Jacopo decided to keep Katrina alive because rumors had it the Vampire Council was coming for her, not to mention since I was her human servant if she happen to die, so would I.

Thomas took over as Alpha of the werewolves. Ever since Antoine was killed there has been total chaos in the pack. Most of them were killed the night of the silver moon either by us or the F.B.I.P.A. The remaining few have been fighting each other for dominance and everything has been total chaos. Thomas decided to step in and try to establish some sort of order and maybe curve their rage into something more positive. He knew his hands would be full, but if he could save a few from their mindless blood lust, it would all be worth it.

Thomas also took Tom under his wing, or paw so to speak. It's been a long hard battle for Tom over the last month. He started working mostly the day shift at Aces Pizza. That way he would have his evenings free. A few nights a week he would spend with Thomas, trying to learn how to better control the lycanthropy. There has been two full moons since the night Tom had been bitten, and each time he transformed. Thomas had him bound with silver chains until he could better control the lycanthropy. This way Tom wouldn't escape and harm someone. I knew he couldn't live with himself if he did. Tom's family has been taking it really hard. Not only did they now know the supernatural does exist, but the head of the house has become one. Also, Tom has become very moody, an uncontrollable part of being a werewolf. Tom's wife and kids love him very much, so they fought to look beyond what has happened, even though they have been forced to stay at a motel on the nights of the full moon. This precaution was just in case Tom ever broke his bonds. Thomas said the first thing Tom would do was follow his instincts and go home. Once there, he would see his family as invaders and slaughter them.

Nothing really changed about Shaun and Danny over the last month. It took a while for Shaun to heal since he didn't have supernatural regeneration, but all his wounds healed up. He has been ordering Aconitum Lycoctonum, an exotic plant about a meter in height with palmate lobed leaves, or more commonly known as wolfsbane. The dark violet flowers on the plant are extremely poisonous if ingested, but to a werewolf it is immediately fatal. We found a way to make a serum which could be injected into a werewolf by means of a tranquilizer dart, it proved very effective.

Danny seems to be coping with his supernatural side. As a matter of fact, I would say he enjoys it very much. He's stronger, faster, rarely gets tired, and never gets sick. Danny changed his schedule at Aces to match Tom's. I guess it was to help him cope with the lycanthropy, or to just keep an eye on him. I've also been working more day shifts. Mostly the same shift Tom and Danny works. I guess Tom wants to keep the three of us in the same loop and away from his normal employees.

Zack seemed to be happier since Katrina's been locked up. Jean Luke is much more patient and forgiving of his minions. Especially since Zack is a free willed vampire, with no master to command him. If he was more powerful, Zack could start a vampire coven of his own. Even though I couldn't picture Zack as a master. He's not serious enough. Having his own coven would just be an excuse to party both day and night. I'm also sure all his servants would be female.

Kiki decided to stay with Jean Luke, mostly because he threatened to hunt her down and kill her if she tried. Jean Luke knew Kiki was powerful enough to start her own coven and he didn't want her as a future rival. Once her coven was powerful enough she would start a war with Jean Luke. If that should ever happen I was sure I would be number one on her hit list. The only thing stopping her from killing me right now, was all my friends. Not only would she have to go through Jean Luke and his vampires, but also Selene and the were-panthers.

Selene finished rebuilding La Luna. It looked really nice once the construction was finished. The repairs took a little over a month. After our battle with the werewolves the restaurant was totally trashed. It cost Selene thousands of dollars to complete the remodel, but with the way it looked when they were finished, it was worth every penny. The big picture windows in the dining area were replaced by a stain glass mural. It was a jungle scene with panthers lying around in trees. It looked very exotic. The old carpet was ripped out and replaced with an expensive forest green vase carpet. It was made in Persia sometime in the Mid-17th century. Selene said she got it a long time ago and had it in storage. When I asked her how long ago, she just smiled and said, "Sometime before you were born." I didn't care for her answer, but it would have been rude to pry.

In the center of the dining room was a bronze statue of a life size panther. I liked the way it looked and I thought it brought a nice atmosphere to the restaurant. The artist brought out every fine detail of the panther, it almost looked alive. Cleo and the other waitresses thought it was in the way and didn't like it.

Selene and I decided to take the next step in our relationship. I sold my house and moved in with her, which was her idea. Selene's house was much bigger than mine, which I had to get used to. I did like the idea of having a fireplace in the dining room. It was romantic in a diner for two sort of way.

Since Selene's house was up on the far South side of town, it took me longer to get to work. I was late sometimes, but in all the years I worked at Aces, no one ever really cared if you were a few minutes late.

Most mornings I forget I made the move to Selene's and freak out when I realize I wasn't in my bed. My senses were always dull when I first wake up in the morning. Then again, I could hardly even qualify as a human in the morning until after my first cup of coffee. Until then I may as well be a zombie. This morning was no different. I forgot to shut the window blinds last night, so I woke this morning with the sun in my eyes. Startled, I instantly sat up in bed, which wasn't a good thing. I didn't know if it was the rude awakening or the early morning fast movement, but my stomach turned. I just made it to the bathroom in time before I retched. A couple moments later I heard a knock at the bathroom door, followed by Selene's voice.

"Are you all right, Jack?" Selene asked and I heard the concern in her voice.

"Yeah," I replied as I wiped my face with a cold, wet towel. "My stomach just turned on me. Must have been what we had for dinner last night."

"You had steak," Selene said and even though diner didn't taste as good coming up as it did going down, my mouth began to water. "Maybe you should let Xylon cook it next time before you decide to eat it."

"You know what I always say," I said and no matter how many times I get sick from doing it, I'll keep doing it, because I love steak. "If it isn't mooing, then I'm not chewing."

For a moment there was no response from the other side of the door, then I heard Selene say, "All right. You just had me worried for a second. Are you sure you're fine?"

"Yeah, I'm all right," I replied and I did feel much better. "I'll be out in a second."

I brushed my teeth and used a little mouth wash to kill the icky vomit taste, then I went back to the bedroom to get dressed. I had to be at work in a couple of hours and wanted to spend a little time with Selene before I did.

Once I was dressed in my Aces hat and shirt I went out to the kitchen. Before I got halfway there I smelt the coffee brewing, it was awesome. I couldn't wait for that first heart starting sip. I could leave the zombie feeling behind and start my day.

Once I entered the kitchen I saw Selene frying up some eggs. I walked up behind her and slid my arms around her waist. She smiled and nuzzled her head under my chin.

"Good morning," I said as I breathed in the sweet aroma of her silky, black hair.

"Good morning to you," Selene replied as she arched her head back to kiss me. "Thank you for using mouth wash."

"I learned from the first time," I said with a laugh as I looked into her beautiful green eyes. "I didn't think you wanted to taste reprocessed diner again."

"No, I didn't," Selene replied with a disgusted look on her face. The last time I kissed her after vomiting was a month ago when I dug up a dead body in the Mineral Palace Park.

After breakfast I finished getting ready for

work. I was just about to walk out the door when my cell phone rang. I looked at the number and saw it was restricted. I almost didn't answer it, but with how weird my life has become, I decided it was probably best if I did. As soon as I answered I heard Agent Jacopo say, "Jack, we have a problem."

"What kind of problem?" I asked, not happy about it involving me. Everything has been very quiet with Katrina gone and I wanted to keep it that way.

"Tyrone busted into the main office last night and freed Katrina," Agent Jacopo replied and my mood became immediately worse. "I don't know how he found us, but he totally surprised the guards. It happen so suddenly no one had a chance to fight back. At least no one was seriously hurt. I was wondering if you heard anything on your end."

"This is the first for me," I replied as Selene walked over to me after noticing my face expression. I knew she could hear everything Agent Jacopo was saying with her supernatural hearing.

"What are you doing right now?" Agent Jacopo asked and something told me I was about to be sent on an errand.

"Getting ready for work," I replied and I hoped that would let me off the hook. "Why do you ask?"

"Once you're off I need you to have a talk with Jean Luke," Agent Jacopo replied and I wasn't happy about that. I didn't mind visiting Jean Luke and Zack, or any of his other minions. It just meant I had to go near Kiki. She's mellowed out a lot since I saved her life during the werewolf fight, but I can tell deep down she still wants me dead. "I need you to talk to him and find out what he knows about the break in, if anything."

"I'll talk to him," I said even though I figured it would be fruitless. "It will be a waste of time, but I'll do it."

"I figure it would be, but I'm not in town right now or I would do it myself," Agent Jacopo said with a sigh. "I'll be stuck up here in the main office for a while and I probably won't be able to make it back down to Pueblo until tomorrow."

"All right," I said with a sigh of my own. "I'll handle it. It's what you guys pay me for anyway."

"Thanks a lot, Jack," Agent Jacopo said and I could hear the stress in his voice. "You know how much getting Katrina back in custody means to me. Anyway, I'll see you tomorrow."

With those words there was a click and the line went dead. I knew exactly how much Agent Jacopo wanted Katrina back. With the Vampire Council looking for her, it was likely they would come to town. If that happens, then he would be able to get the revenge he desires.

Agent Jacopo has been hunting down the supernatural for the last five years. He and his partner were up in Detroit, about to bust a big time drug dealer named Antonio Vesuvius. Everything went as planned until they tried to arrest him.
Agent Jacopo's partner cuffed Antonio and to their amazement he snapped the handcuffs like they were made of cheap plastic.

Antonio's eyes began to glow red, then a moment later he ripped out Agent Jacopo's partner's throat. Petrified and unable to move, Agent Jacopo was unable to defend himself as Antonio bit into his neck and slowly drained away his life force. He would have joined his partner in death if back up didn't arrive right in time. That's when Agent Jacopo found out the supernatural exists and why they never saw Antonio during the day.

Antonio Vesuvius wasn't only a very

powerful vampire, but also one of the five founding members of the Vampire Council. Which is the reason why Agent Jacopo wants Katrina back in custody. With the Vampire Council coming for her, Antonio Vesuvius will be with them, then his partner's death will be avenged.

In the end Agent Jacopo and I want to find and keep Katrina alive, even though it is for different reasons. He wants her as bait and I just want to stay alive.

Once I hung up with Agent Jacopo, Selene looked at me and asked, "Do you want me to come with you? I just have a couple things to do at La Luna, then I can meet you at Aces."

"That sounds good to me," I replied, not wanting to run into Kiki without backup. The last time I did she sent me flying into a wall. My jaw hurt for a week after that punch. "I should be off by 7:00 PM."

I finished getting ready for work, then after a world famous Jack Holladay goodbye kiss, I was out the door. It was a warm day for late October, so I put the top down on my convertible Chevy Camaro. There was nothing like riding in a convertible. Wind blowing through your hair, the sun baking you like an old piece of bacon. It was great. The gas millage was nowhere near as sufficient as my old car, but my Camaro had the power the other car was lacking. Let's see a werewolf catch me in this baby.

Fifteen minutes later I pulled into the Aces parking lot. I saw Tom and Danny's cars, so I parked next to them. As I walked up to the store I saw Danny Perry come out with a delivery. Danny is a rather cool headed and intelligent individual that has an interest in martial arts and playing the piano, he excels at both of them. He has long black hair, which he keeps pulled back into a tail and brown eyes. He isn't very tall, maybe around five feet six inches, but I saw some of his karate and I wouldn't want to mess with him. The height probably came from the oriental side of his family.

Danny's mom met a United States naval officer while he was overseas. The two hit it off and then soon after Danny's father went back to the States. Nine months later Danny was born, but his mother couldn't afford to take care of a baby so she dropped him off at a military base. From there he was put in an orphanage until he was adopted by an American couple.

A couple months back a vampire named Nathaniel abducted Danny and forced me to watch as he went through the process of turning him into a vampire. During the procedure something went wrong and Danny was only half turned, becoming a vampyr. With the transformation he acquired extraordinary strength and speed. He became what all vampires wanted to be. A superhuman that can walk around in the sunlight and doesn't have to survive off humans, although once in a while they do get the craving for rare meat.

"Daaack!" Danny yelled as he saw me walking towards Aces. It was a nickname he gave me and like most nicknames at Aces, it took.

"D-man!" I yelled back. Which was the nickname that I and practically everyone else at Aces had for him. "How's it going?"

"Just another day in Aces paradise," Danny replied and I laughed. "I heard you moved in with Selene. How's that working out for you?"

"What could be better?" I replied with a question. I hate when people do that. "I get to go home every night to the most beautiful woman I ever had the pleasure of meeting. What can I say? How did that old song go? This must be just like living in paradise."

"Yeah, but you're paradise has vampires and lycanthropes in it," Danny said as he put the delivery in his car. "Personally, that's a couple things I could do without."

"You know what they say," I said as Danny

got in his car. "One man's paradise is another ones bloodsucking nightmare."

Danny just shook his head, then laughed and drove off. I walked up to Aces and as soon as I opened the door I saw Tom pulling a pizza out of the oven.

Tom is a decent enough employer. He is willing to work with his employees. If you needed a day off it was usually easy to get, usually.

Tom has a pale complexion and blue eyes, much like me. His blond hair was always neatly trimmed and his clothes were clean and ironed. My hair on the other hand was dark blond and shoulder length. It wasn't messy, but neat also wasn't a word I would use for it. My clothes usually looked like I dragged them out of the hamper, stains and all.

"What's up Kaun?" I asked, calling Tom by a personal nickname I had for him. Unless an employee was a long timer at Aces they wouldn't have a clue who I was talking about. He earned his nickname one day when he arrived at the shop with a personal sized serving of spicy cucumbers. He picked it up at a Chinese restaurant named Kaun's. The rest of the night he ate the cucumbers as he walked around saying, "Tom's Kans." From that night on I started calling him Kaun and the name took.

"Not bad, Jack," Tom replied as he cut the pizza into slices. "How are things going with you?"

I wanted to say, "Just another day in paradise," but as of lately Tom's life has been anything other than perfect, so I decided to say, "Nothing much. Just another day at Aces Pizza."

Tom just looked at me for a moment, then laughed. For a moment it was like old times. If I didn't know Tom was a werewolf, I would never have guessed. He seemed to be adjusting and hiding it well.

"So how are things with Selene?" Tom asked and he didn't have to say it, because I could already tell what he was thinking. It was the same thing everybody was thinking. How did I get a sexy, charming, and sophisticated woman to fall for me? It wasn't my income, because I was always broke. It wasn't my looks, because I was average at best. As for my personality, it was kind of dull. I never know what to say, so I just tell everyone that Selene is into guys who are poor, average looking, and dull.

"So far it's been great," I replied as I clocked in for the day. "Moving in with her is taking a little getting used to, but besides that, it's been awesome."

"I guess that first night you're car broke down and the vampire attacked you, it kind of worked out for the best," Tom said, and ironically, if it wasn't for that fateful night, my life would be totally different right now. Much less exciting and fulfilling. "Also, now that Katrina is locked up and out of the picture, you can get on with your life."

"Ummm, about Katrina," I said and Tom just looked at me. "She kind of escaped her holding cell and no one knows where she is."

"That's not good," Tom said with a worried tone to his voice. "Do you think she will come after you?"

"I'm doubtful about it," I replied in my best reassuring voice. I didn't need Tom to worry about her. He already has enough on his plate. "I'm going out to the mansion tonight after work and talk to Jean Luke. I'm sure he'll know what to do."

"More vampire business," Tom said with a bitter tone to his voice. I knew he didn't like the idea of me hanging around with them. "I guess you can't escape you're curse any more than I can mine."

With those words Tom fell silent. I know

being a werewolf is hard on him. It's been hard on his whole family. His older daughter enrolled into college and a couple weeks back she left for Tennessee. There was talk about her attending the University here in Pueblo, but after what happened to Tom, I guess she figured it was easier to deal with from several hundred miles away. I didn't blame her, and neither did Tom.

Absentmindedly, Tom set the pizza down in front of me, then walked away. He didn't say anything, but I knew he intended for me to deliver it. I put the pizza in a delivery bag and headed out the door.

The rest of the day went the same way. It wasn't very busy and Tom didn't feel like talking. I spent most of our down time talking to Danny or wondering what I was going to do about Katrina. I told Danny about her and as long as she kept her distance, he could care less. Personally, I think Danny could take Katrina in a fight.

Time crept on until the closing crew came in around 4:00pm. Frank was the first to show up. He's one of the three assistant managers and I guess if we had a chain of command, he would be second. Frank is one of those people who can eat his body weight and never gain a pound. It is totally sick on how much he can eat at a sitting and in the ten years I knew him he never put on any weight. He was just the same old Frank. Kind of nerdy looking with his short black hair parted to the side and big framed glasses, but he was tall and kind of muscular. Anytime I would walk in late he would look at me and say, "Well, well, well, look who decided to show up." Then he would slug me in the arm or leg. He always was a little aggressive.

Shortly after Frank, Robert walked in. As soon as I saw him I walked up and asked, "What's up, Roberto?"

"Nothing much," Robert replied as he walked over to the computer and clocked in. "I picked up a couple new pieces for my Halloween costume. It's looking really awesome."

If there was such a thing as a nice guy award, Robert would be most likely to win it. He was always doing favors for people. I guess his big heart came from being such a big guy. He stood about six foot and weighed roughly three hundred pounds. Like Frank, Robert also wore glasses. He has long brown hair, which he keeps tied back in a tail and a full facial beard. I seen Robert once without his beard, he definitely looks better with it. Either that or I was just used to seeing him with it.

This year for Halloween Robert is dressing up as a vigilante from one of the comics he reads.

He already picked up the smiley face button from a comic convention and a couple realistic looking plastic guns. They were kind of cool, the clips even came out. Robert loved Halloween. He said he and his wife were pagans so it was part of their religion. He celebrated Halloween like other people celebrated Christmas. One day he told me about Wicca. It was kind of weird, but I guess at least he's not running naked around Stonehenge while chasing a chicken with a dagger.

After Robert finished describing his costume to me, the phone began to ring. It looked like we were going to be busy after all. I made another five deliveries and once I returned from the last one I saw Selene's car parked in the lot. I looked in her car as I walked by and didn't see her. I figured she was inside.

As soon as I opened the door I saw Selene sitting at one of the tables, talking to Tom. I didn't know what they were talking about, but I figured it was one of two things, me or Tom's lycanthropy.

Once I walked through the door Selene smiled at me and Tom made the same gesture an umpire would to a batter after striking out. At the same time he said, "You're out of here."

As I walked towards the office Frank got my delivery money out of the drop box. Not many drivers actually keep their money in there, but I always have. I don't like having two or three hundred dollars on me or in my car. I'm responsible for every penny, if I lose it I have to pay it back.

I started to count the cash in my pocket as Frank came into the office with the rest. He purposefully bumped into me, then he playfully said, "Watch it, Jack. You don't want any of this."

"Nobody wants any of that," I replied as I laid my money on the desk. "I don't think even you're wife wants any of that."

Frank slugged me in the leg and for a brief moment it became numb and gave out. I stumbled, but didn't fall. I looked at him and said, "Dork."

"Look who's talking," Frank said as a smile snaked across his face. "I still don't see what Selene sees in you. She's beautiful and you're-- you."

"Well, I guess that's the part she likes," I said and Frank just shook his head.

Once Frank was finished cashing me out I went out front to meet Selene. Tom was back tending to the ovens so I waved to him as I headed to the exit.

"Let me know how things go," Tom said as I opened the door.

"I will," I replied as Selene and I walked out into the night. We strolled across the parking lot we reached our cars. We decided to drop Selene's off at home and take the Camaro.

Once we were home I changed out of my Aces uniform and fastened on my ankle holster. I loaded my .380 with wood bullets and strapped it in the holster. Next I put on my leather trench coat and strapped in the 16 gauge shotgun. You couldn't see it unless I pulled open the trench. I learned in the past to never visit vampires without some type of weapon. It's not that I didn't trust Jean Luke, I just didn't want to have my jaw nearly broken by Kiki again.

Once I was changed and armed we started on our way to the mansion. The sky was clear and the moon was bright. The air had a nip to it, but it was still relatively warm for October. I did put the top back up on the Camaro. The last thing I needed to do was catch a cold, especially since I had to deal with vampires. With my vomiting episode this morning I was already feeling drained the way it was. No pun intended.

Selene looked at me, she could tell I was

nervous. She put her hand on my leg and as I glanced over at her, she smiled. I knew if Kiki started anything, Selene would have my back.

Chapter Two

As we drove down the street towards the mansion I saw the beginning of the cast iron fence which surrounded it. The top of the fence was tipped and looked razor sharp. I followed the fence to the driveway, which was blocked by a gate. I stopped at the gate and pushed the button on the intercom. A couple moments later the familiar voice of the butler asked, "Hello, how may I be of service?"

"It's Jack, Jarvis," I said after pushing the button on the intercom. "I've come to have a word with Jean Luke."

"Master Jack, what a nice surprise," Jarvis said as I heard the gates start to squeak and grind as they opened. "Please, come in. I'll inform Master Jean Luke you are here and wish to speak with him."

As soon as the gates were open I drove through and up the long road to the mansion. The mansion was enormous and there were trees all around so it was completely sealed from the main road. Unless you were looking for it, there was no way of knowing it existed.

The estate was beautiful. It had three floors, with grand picture windows in the front. There were thick curtains on the windows so I couldn't see inside. The outside walls were white stucco, with black trim.

The grounds were gorgeously landscaped. All the ornate landscaping was once full of luscious green grass the last time I was here, but since it was the beginning of fall only patches of green still existed. Well maintained bushes lined halfway down both sides of the outer wall, but the flowers which bloomed down the sides of the sidewalk have shriveled up, not to bloom again until spring. The mansion looked like a celebrity house that would be seen on TV or on the cover of a home magazine, not something belonging to a vampire.

I got out of my car and waited for Selene, then together we walked up to the mansion. I knocked on the door and a few moments later it opened.

I saw Jarvis standing in front of us wearing a tuxedo. His black hair was balding and his nose stuck up as he stared at me with black beady eyes. He was tall, at least six foot three inches and very skinny. He almost looked like a skeleton with skin.

He had a snobbish air about him, even though I knew he wasn't. I knew it was all an act for the vampires who resided in the mansion. Jarvis was Shaun's informant and old friend. Besides Shaun, only Selene and I knew this secret, and we would take it with us to our graves.

"Come in, Master Holladay and Madam Selene," Jarvis said as he stared at us from under bushy eyebrows. "Master Jean Luke is waiting for you in the living room."

We stepped in and Jarvis closed the door. The large sitting area we were standing in was completely paneled in dark wood. There were several pieces of Victorian style furniture in this room. In the middle of the room were two loveseats and four comfortable looking chairs surrounding a coffee table.

Only one painting adorned the walls in this room. It was an ocean scene. When I look at it I find it breathtaking with all the vibrant colors in the sky. In the foreground was an old ship, possibly a galleon. The ship looked to glide across the waves with the wind in its sails. In the background was either the rising or the setting of the sun.

"Please follow me," Jarvis said as he began to walk down a hallway leading away from the sitting room.

We followed Jarvis down the hall to the living room and I immediately sensed supernatural from the other side of the door. Jarvis opened the door and stood to the side as Selene and I walked past him and into the room.

As soon as I entered my attention was immediately drawn to Kiki. She was stretched across a loveseat in a half-sitting position. Her long, blond hair was tied up into piggy tails. Her girlish, innocent look was only betrayed by the sinister look in her blue eyes. She wore a tight pink halter top that left little to the imagination and a short, short red mini skirt. She topped off her outfit with spiked-heeled red leather boots that came up to the top of her calves. The vampire smiled at me when I saw her, showing off her fangs. I did my best to ignore Kiki, but that just made her smile wider. Every time I see her smug face over the last month I wondered why I saved her life during the battle with the werewolves.

A comfortable looking sectional sat on the other side of the love seat. The two pieces of furniture surrounded a seventy-two inch big screen TV, which was mounted on the wall.

Sitting on the sectional was Tabitha. She ran her fingers through her long blond hair as she stared at me with blue eyes. Tabitha didn't look any more than eighteen, but I knew when it came to vampires, looks were very deceiving. She wore a flowery summer dress, which only made her look younger and innocent. She topped off the outfit with white heeled shoes.

Terrance was sitting in the middle of the sectional, talking to Zack, who was sitting next to him. Terrance was handsome, with short black hair and green eyes. He wore a blue dress shirt and black slacks, with a red tie.

Zack had long blond hair that was short and kind of spiky on top. He wore ripped blue jeans and a plain white sleeveless t-shirt. Between his hair and the clothes he wore he looked like some kind of teenage rocker from the nineteen eighties generation.

The last person in the room was Jean Luke. He looked to be in his mid-twenties, but his blue eyes implied he was much older. Jean Luke was ruggedl y handsome with his long, straight, blond hair and neatly trimmed goatee.

Jean Luke was standing over by one of the picture windows, staring out into the night. I knew he was thinking about Elizabeth, because he looked the same way the night she died. I felt sorry for him. I've had a couple friends die recently, but not a lover, and most certainly not someone I have known and loved for centuries.

Selene and I started to walk across the room towards Jean Luke, but before we got a few steps, Zack looked over his shoulder and saw us. Once he did he said, "Jack is in the house. What's up, Holladay?"

"How's it going, Zack?" I asked and at that moment all eyes were on us. "We just stopped by to have a few words with Jean Luke."

"I thought you came all the way out here to see me," Zack said with a feigned hurt expression on his face. "What's wrong, Jack? Don't you love me anymore?"

With those words Zack leaped off the couch and using his vampire speed, he was instantly in front of me. Before I could do anything Zack engulfed me in a bear hug and said, "I haven't seen you in weeks. You don't call. You don't write. I was starting to think you didn't care, but that's all right. I forgive you. Give me a kiss."

I tried to pull away from Zack, but my effort was in vain. Zack could bench press a car. I could probably lift 160 pounds on a good day. The chances of me breaking his embrace was nil at best. With all my effort, I still got a big, sloppy vampire kiss on my forehead. Everybody laughed, but me. Even Jean Luke smiled. It was nice to see him do so after all he has been through.

Once Zack was finished he released me, then he looked at Selene and said, "You're turn." Selene just stared at Zack and the look on her face said, "Touch me and I'll scratch you're eyes out." After seeing that look, Zack had second thoughts and said, "Or not."

It was my turn to laugh.

Once Zack was finished having his fun we approached Jean Luke. The vampire turned from the window and stared at Selene and me. His eyes were void of expression and have been that way since the night Elizabeth died. Jean Luke loved her and she was killed while saving my life. I don't know if Jean Luke blamed me for her death, but one thing was for sure, things have not been the same since that tragic occurrence.

"Welcome back, Jack," Jean Luke said as he politely extended his hand in welcome. "Ya haven't been around much since our battle wit te werewolves."

"Yeah, I know," I said as I shook his hand. "I don't usually hang around places which can potentially be hazardous to my health."

"No one here wishes to harm ya, Jack," Jean Luke said, then I gestured towards Kiki, who was staring at me with a big smile. "Ya are my friend, Jack. Kiki would not dare lay a hand on ya. She knows if she did, it would lead ta her death, and it would not be swift."

I knew Kiki could hear our whole conversation. It must drive her insane to know she can't touch me. So what I did next I knew I really shouldn't have done. I looked at Kiki, making full eye contact since I knew vampire hypnotism had no effect on me, and smiled. Her eyes glowed red for a moment and her smile vanished. I was beginning to enjoy myself until Selene gave my arm a gentle squeeze, then whispered in my ear, "Don't tease the animals."

I laughed at her comment. I wasn't sure if Kiki heard it or not, even with her vampire hearing. At that time her gaze left me and went to Selene, then I knew. I couldn't help myself, but laugh again. Selene ignored Kiki, which made matters worse. The vampire got up from her seat and stormed out of the room, while all along, not taking her gaze off me and Selene.

Once Kiki left the room, Jean Luke smiled and said, "Tat went well. Now A'm sure yer here fer somting, because ya never stop by just ta chat. What can ah do for ya, Jack?"

"I was wondering if you heard about Katrina and Tyrone." I asked, hoping that Jean Luke wasn't involved in Katrina's jail break. Tyrone broke into the facility where they were holding Katrina and freed her."

Jean Luke's face expression grew stern, then he turned back to the picture window and stared out into the darkness. Whatever he was staring at I couldn't see, if he was staring at anything at all. For a few moments there was silence, then he said, "Tyrone has been missing for days. A'm not his master, so ah don't have any control over him, or know where he is. Ah do know tat when Katrina was apprehended Tyrone was not happy and has been very moody ever since. Ah decided ta give him room until he came around. Ah never taught he would do somting so drastic."

"I'm sure Katrina's going to want revenge on me for setting her up," I said and the thought wasn't pleasant. "Not to mention, stripping her of all her minions."

"Tiss true, Mon ami," Jean Luke agreed as he faced us again. "Ya did weaken her a lot. A vampire isn't a master without servants and a human servant. You're probably te only power source she has left, and ya would have ta die before she could get another. Your life is definitely in danger."

"Great," I said, not liking the idea of being on a vampire's hit list again. "When will all of this be over? When will I be able to live a normal life without someone, or something wanting to kill me?"

"Hence te life tat was thrown upon ya, Mon ami," Jean Luke replied as he put his hand on my shoulder and looked me in the eyes. "A'm sorry, Jack, but as long as ya live in te world of te supernatural, your life will never be normal. If ya want ah can make sure ya have continual protection every night from dusk till dawn."

"He already has that, Jean Luke," Selene said and it was true. I would rather that Selene have my back than a vampire any day. Not that I don't trust Jean Luke's vampires, except for Kiki anyway. It's just, I've seen Selene in a fight and it was very impressive. "I was more than a challenge for Katrina, even before she lost her minions."

"Point well taken, chere," Jean Luke said with a smile. "A've never underestimated your power, or te power of your Pride. Ah just want ta make sure Jack is safe."

"Even though Selene may not need us," Tabitha said as she stood from her seat and walked over to us. "I will help her keep an eyes on Jack."

"Same here, man," Zack said as he walked over and put his hand on my shoulder. "Jack and I are bro's. He broke Katrina's hold over me. She would have to go through me to get to him."

"Don't underestimated her, mon amie," Jean Luke said with a little tinge of warning in his voice. "Even in her weaken state Katrina is more tan a match for ya."

"I'll contact Agent Jacopo and let him know that you haven't heard from Katrina," I said and there was a lot of looks among the vampires. "I'll also let him know that she may be coming after me."

Agent Jacopo wasn't liked much by the vampire community. He wanted the vampires dead, but right now they served his purpose. The Vampire Council was on its way to put Katrina on trial for the war against Nathaniel, and one of the Council members was Antonio Vesuvius. Agent Jacopo despised this bloodsucker more than any other. Mostly, because it killed his partner and left him for dead.

"Be careful with Agent Jacopo," Jean Luke said and I heard the sound of urgency in his voice. "Don't let his desire for revenge be your undoing.

Antonio Vesuvius is his fight, not yours."

"If Antonio wants Katrina dead, then it is my fight," I said, feeling even more dread. Katrina wants me dead, but Antonio wants her dead. Either way, it don't sound good for me. "We all know what happens to me if Antonio finds Katrina first."

"Katrina will be put on trial first, mon ami," Jean Luke said, which made me feel a little better, but the next part did not. "Once Antonio has Katrina he will ten send for ya. Since ya are her human servant, her fate will also be yours."

"Great," I said, my heart sinking. "Then why am I wasting time here? I need to get out there so she can find me before Antonio finds her."

"Tat's going ta be dangerous, mon ami," Jean Luke said and anymore I really didn't care. I just wanted this over with. If keeping Katrina locked up and out of the clutches of Antonio was the way for it to happen, then I was going to make sure it did.

"I don't care anymore, Jean Luke," I said as I started to walk towards the door. "I just want this over with and if using myself as bait is a way of doing it, then so be it. If you guys want to help, great, we can use it. If not, then that is fine also. It's not your fight, but if I never see you again, then goodbye and watch your backs."

By the time I got to the front door of the mansion I was regretting my decision to use myself as bait, but something needed to be done. I opened the door and walked out into the night. With Selene by my side we made our way over to the car, but before we reached it I sensed supernatural. I turned to face Kiki and when I did I got hit in the face. I didn't know what it was that hit me, but it shattered on impact and stung like no other. A couple small shards got in my eyes, blinding me momentarily. Selene began to growl, then I heard Kiki say, "Back off, Pussy Cat. Jack's not hurt, just his pride. Not unless that little pine-cone was more than he could handle."

"What do you want, Kiki?" I asked as I rubbed my eyes. They watered like crazy, but at least my vision was starting to clear.

"First, I want you and this feline to keep your traps shut," Kiki replied and my vision cleared enough to see the vampire and Selene were face to face, and the tension in the air was thick. "Second, I want her face out of mine."

"Back off, Selene," I said, but the were-panther didn't back down. "Let's hear what she has to say."

Selene took a couple steps back, but she was still in striking distance. I knew she wanted to rip out Kiki's throat, and I would love to watch her do it. But this time the vampire was right, we did start it. For once Kiki did not make the first move. I didn't say anything for a couple moments until my vision completely cleared, then I said, "Alright, Kiki. Let's hear what you have to say."

"I want a truce between us," Kiki said and I couldn't hide the amused look on my face. "As you know the Vampire Council is coming and as of right now I am a rogue vampire. If I don't have a master or a coven of my own before the Council gets here, they will kill me."

"Why don't you just join Jean Luke's coven?" I asked, kind of hoping in a way that the Council would show up right now.

"He won't allow me to join until I make amends with you," Kiki replied and I couldn't help it, I laughed. "Laugh all you want, Jack. Everyone knows I did when Jean Luke told me what had to be done. I figured I would have my own coven by now, but I'm not strong enough. I couldn't make a human servant. Every time I tried he would die and it's not easy to find someone who is willing to become a vampire's human servant.

"Why don't you just force someone like

Katrina forced me?" I asked while remembering that unfortunate day a few months back.

"Because if you force someone to become your human servant you will lose control over them," Kiki replied and things started to make sense. "Which is the reason why Katrina wasn't able to dominate and control you. Not to mention, even if I forced someone to become my human servant, they would die during the ritual anyway. I'm still not powerful enough to be a master. So the only way I will survive the Council's visit is to join Jean Luke's coven and in order for that to happen I need to make amends with you."

I thought about it for a while and figured if I really wanted Kiki dead I could have let it happen during the werewolf battle. I knew Kiki was impatient and I just wanted to start my search for Katrina. I took a deep breath and let it out slowly, then said, "I suppose we can let by gones be by gones. I just hope I don't regret it."

At that time I saw Kiki smile and for the first time it didn't have a dagger strapped onto it. Then, in a blink of the eye, Kiki was gone. I figured she went into the mansion to tell Jean Luke what happened. I looked at Selene and she was staring at me with a curious look. I just shrugged, then walked over and got into my car. Once Selene was in I drove away from the mansion, in search of Katrina, the person I never wanted to see again.

Chapter Three

We headed back home. On the way there the only thing I could think about was finding Katrina before the Vampire Council does. I still don't know how the whole human servant thing works. The servant dying because the master was killed doesn't make any sense to me. Then again, hanging around with vampires and fighting werewolves doesn't either. The only thing I do know is I have never been happier than I am right now with Selene, and I don't intend to let a bunch of bloodsuckers ruin that.

About twenty minutes later we pulled into the drive-way. For a moment I just sat there, looking off into the darkness. Then I felt Selene's hand on my leg. I looked at her and she smiled at me, then she said, "Are we going inside? I'm fine with staying out here in the car, but for what I have in mind I think the bed would be much more comfortable."

I smiled at Selene and I guess the look on my face was goofy , because she laughed. I opened the car door and got out. Nothing looked out of the ordinary, but as I started to walk up to the house I sensed supernatural. I knew it wasn't coming from Selene, so as I looked around I motioned to her. Once she saw me the were-panther was instantly on guard. A moment later Tyrone stepped out of the shadows.

Tyrone used to be a bouncer at the Crimson Chateau before it burned down a few months ago. He also used to be one of Katrina's servants until I broke the bond she held over him. She never forgave me for that, even though Tyrone decided to stay with her.

Tyrone was tall, at least six feet and he was extremely muscular. His skin was very dark to the point I almost didn't see him in the dim light. His head was shaved and when he spoke he had a very low voice.

"Hey, Jacky boy," Tyrone said, which made me jump a little and Selene tensed up as she prepared to defend me. "Hold on, Selene. I'm not here for a fight. I just want to talk."

"So talk," Selene said, not relaxing one bit. "But if you even flinch I will tear out your throat before you take two steps towards Jack."

"I wouldn't hurt Jack, Selene," Tyrone said, and even though Selene didn't believe him, I did. "He's saved my life before and for the last few months he has been a good friend."

"What do you want then?" Selene asked, still not trusting the big vampire. "And where is that blood sucking fiend you call a master?"

"Katrina is why I'm here," Tyrone replied and I was happy my search for her was going to be easier than what I expected. "She sent me to find you."

"Where's Katrina, Tyrone," I asked and the big vampire just stared at me. "With the Council on the way here..."

"The Vampire Council is already here," Tyrone interrupted and we just stared at him. "They arrived last night and have been searching for Katrina ever since. We have been keeping tabs on them and found out they are also looking for you."

"Actually," a voice I didn't recognize said from behind me. "We just found him."

I sensed supernatural as Selene and I turned to see four men in their late teens to early twenties step out of the shadows. The one who spoke had short black hair, which was neatly trimmed. He wore a dress shirt and black jeans. He also looked to be the oldest of the four men.

The one next to him had long, curly brown hair. He wore a black T-shirt and blue jeans. He just stood there, staring at us with a cocky smirk on his face.

The third of the group had short, messy blond hair and looked younger than the other two men. He wore a gray hoodie and blue jeans.

The last of the vampires had short, wavy black hair. He wore a striped polo and blue jeans. He looked to be the youngest of the group and stood behind the others.

"My name is David and I represent my master, Antonio Vesuvius. You're a hard person to find, Jack," the vampire said as I pulled my .380 out of its holster. "Now that's rude, Jack. Were just here to invite you to a meeting. Your little friends are invited as well. I advice you all to come peacefully, but I understand if you don't comply."

"You can take your invitation and shove it," I said as I chambered a bullet. "I'm not interested in your meetings or anything you bloodsuckers have to say."

"I was hoping you would say that," David said with a smile that showed a good deal of fang. "Have at them, boys. But remember, the master wants Jack and Tyrone alive. The were-panther is mine. I have my own reasons for her."

The other vampires laughed as they began to flank out. I knew they were trying to surround us, so I put my back to Selene's as she transformed into her hybrid form. Seeing her like that always made me uncomfortable; the face of a cat and a body of a human with three inch long claws. It was unnerving for me, but she was very formidable in that form.

Tyrone vamped out, brandishing his fangs. He hissed as the vampire with the long, curly brown hair made a fake lunge at him. The vampire laughed as he began to circle us again.

I aimed at the vampire with the short blond hair and was about to squeeze off a shot, but he lunged at me. I knew he was using his vampire speed. I shouldn't have been able to see him, but I did. Thanks to one of the abilities I received from the numerous bites by Katrina, I was able to keep up with the vampire. To me he was moving like a normal human. Once the vampire was close enough I fired, but at the last moment he must have noticed I could follow his everything move, because he jerked to the right. Instead of a killing blow to the heart I ended up shooting him in the shoulder. Because of his last moment dodge and the force of the bullet, the vampire spun around before falling to the ground. The vampire clutched his shoulder as he grimaced in pain. I took aim again, this time I didn't plan on missing. Just before I pulled the trigger the vampire wearing the polo clawed my hand, drawing blood and making me drop my gun. I clenched my hand as blood began to flow from the wound. The gashes looked deep. Great. More stitches.

Seeing I was in trouble, Selene turned to help me. The were-panther was about to rip out the vampire's throat, but before she could strike, David grabbed her from behind, pinning her arms to her chest. Selene struggled to break free, but the vampire was stronger than her.

Seeing we were at a disadvantage the vampire with the long brown hair lunged at Tyrone again. The big vampire tried to dodge the blow, but it connected, leaving deep gashes on his cheek. Tyrone countered with a strike of his own. Claws slashed the vampire's chest, ripping his T-shirt and the flesh underneath. The vampire's hand went to his chest and when he pulled it away it was drenched with blood. Tyrone's attack had cut deep.

Seeing Selene couldn't help me I went for the shotgun in my trench. The weapon was heavy so I couldn't get it out fast enough before the vampire wearing the polo grabbed my arm and squeezed. Pain shot up my arm and throughout my body as I dropped the shotgun. I let out a scream as I felt things begin to crack. Any more pressure and my arm would break, the bone would puncture through my skin. The vampire had me completely at his mercy. Using my arm he forced me to the ground. I was helpless and in an immense amount of pain. I felt as if I would wretch at any moment.

The only one of us who could do anything was Tyrone. He was winning the fight with the other vampire and probably could have finished him off if it wasn't for David. While holding Selene in submission he looked at Tyrone and said, "Give it up, Tyrone, or I'll have Marko snap Jack's arm."

At that time Marko applied a little pressure on my arm, making me cry out again. Tyrone looked over at me. He saw how much pain I was in and even though he wanted to give in to his blood lust and keep fighting, the big vampire lowered his defenses and bowed his head.

Just when I thought it was over and we had lost the fight, Zack and Tabitha came out of nowhere. The two vampire's attacks were so fast and quiet, David and his gang never saw it coming. Zack attacked Marko, breaking his grip on my arm and then breaking three of his fingers. It was now Marko's turn to cry out.

At the same time Tabitha slammed into David's back, throwing him off guard and breaking his grip on Selene. The were-panther didn't hesitate for a moment. She spun around and clawed David across the face. The vampire screamed as his hands went to his face. Blood gushed from the wound, covering his fingers.

Seeing that they were now outnumbered and hurt badly, David yelled, "The fun is over, boys! Let's get out of here!"

With those words the four vampires were instantly gone, but even though they were nowhere to be seen I could still hear David's voice, as if it was blowing in on the wind, "This isn't over, Jack."

Once Selene was sure David and the other vampires were gone, she came over to check on me. The first thing she looked at was my arm. She moved it around, which hurt like heck. Fortunately, it wasn't broke. It was just going to be sore for the next few days. Next, she checked out the gashes in my hand. After examining it she looked at me and said, "This is going to need stitches."

"I had a feeling about that," I said with a sigh. "Damn it! I hate needles!"

Everyone stopped what they were doing and

stared at me. They were all thinking the same thing, but it was Zack who said it. "Wow! Jack just let out the big "D" word. I think this is the first time I have ever heard you swear."

"Yeah," I said, not liking the fact that everyone was staring at me. "It just kind of slipped out."

"Slipped?" Zack said with a laugh. "That sucker exploded like a race horse out of the gate."

"That's enough, Zack," Selene said as she stared at me with concern in her eyes. "With everything which has been going on I think he is entitled to at least one."

"Were those guys from the Vampire Council?" Zack asked and I nodded. "Great. So much for first impressions. I guess it was a good thing Jean Luke sent me and Tabitha to keep an eye on you. Hey, Tyrone. How's it going? Katrina's not nearby, is she?"

"Considering the circumstances, I am doing fine, and you have nothing to worry about, Katrina isn't here," Tyrone replied and Zack let out a sigh of relief. "Speaking of Katrina, I need to get back to her. I wasn't supposed to be gone this long. She sent me to give you a message, Jack. She wants to talk to you."

"Well, I want to speak to her as well," I said and I was happy she was making my search for her very easy. "When and where does she want to meet?"

"Tomorrow night," Tyrone replied, then a smile snaked across his face and he chuckled. "The same place you killed Boris."

"The graveyard?" I asked and I couldn't hide how surprised I was; then Tyrone nodded as his smile grew larger. "Why there?"

"I'm not exactly sure," Tyrone replied and his smile faded a little. "Maybe this is her way of starting over; making amends for everything which happened. You will have to talk to her to find out."

"Fine," I said, not sharing Tyrone's smile. "I'll be there.

"I'm not saying I don't trust Tyrone," Tabitha said as she looked at the big vampire, then over to me. "I just think Zack and I should go with you to this meeting. We don't know what she has planned and backup wouldn't be a bad idea."

"I think your right," I said and Tyrone's smile faded all together. "It's not that I don't trust you, Tyrone. I just think with the Vampire Council being in town, a little back up would be nice. I don't want another surprise like tonight."

"Wait a second," Zack said and I could tell by the look on his face, he didn't like the plan. "I agree with back-up. That's a good idea, but why do I have to be part of it. I don't want to see Katrina again. Let's don't forget, she probably wants me dead. I don't want to be turned into a little black Zack pebble."

"Wussy," Tyrone said with a smile as he looked at Zack. "You have been a vampire for almost forty years. Its time you grew a pair."

"Fine," Zack said and he didn't look happy at all. "I'll go, but if I get killed, my little pebble ass is going to come back and haunt you. I'll roll into your coffin one morning and you'll sleep on me all day, then that night you will have a horrible back pain."

Tyrone just laughed and I couldn't help myself, I did as well. Then all the laughter stopped as we saw lights and heard sirens heading our way. Someone must have heard the gun shot and called the police."

"You guys had better vanish," I said and the vampires were instantly gone. Selene and I waited outside for the police. Once they arrived I flashed my FBI badge and took over the crime scene. I told the police some punks were trying to rob us and I shot one after having my hand torn up. They bought the story and the evidence around the yard proved it. An ambulance arrived, just in case anyone was hurt. They stitched up my hand and once everything calmed down, Selene and I went inside to get cleaned up. There was a lot of excitement tonight and needless to say, I didn't get much sleep.

Chapter Four

That night I had a disturbing dream. David and his three goons circled me with fangs bared. I tried to run from them, but no matter where I went, there they were. While this was happening a shadow loomed over me, like a dark lord over-seeing his devious plans.

The vampires pursued me through dark alleys until I came to a dead-end. I had nowhere else to run as they slowly advanced towards me like predators stalking their prey. Then in a blink of the eye they were upon me, their claws tearing at my flesh. I screamed over and over, but no help came.

That was when I woke from my dream, screaming. It was then I found out part of the dream was real. It was pitch dark in the room and my awareness was still kind of hazy from being rapidly awoken from my sleep. I still felt the vampires ripping at my flesh, and to my alarm it was real. Someone loomed above me, tearing at me with bone like claws.

Since I was sleeping on my left side and

covered by a thick quilt, the cuts on my arm were only surface deep. I tried to free myself from my attackers grasp, but he had me pinned beneath the quilt.

Selene was awoken by my scream and she reacted much faster than I did. The were-panther lunged at my assailant, transforming into her hybrid form in the process. Using her supernatural strength and amazing agility, Selene was able to knock the attacker off me and land on her feet, ready to strike again.

I took the opportunity to roll out of bed. I fumbled for the lamp, since it seemed I was the only person in the room who couldn't see in the dark. With a burst of light, everyone was stunned for just a moment. Now the playing field was a little more even, I saw my assailant. I finally had my wits about me and time to focus, I finally sensed supernatural a moment before I saw his face. It was Alan Shoemaker.

"Shoe?" I asked as I looked at my dearly departed friend. "Is it really you?"

I was in complete shock. The person standing in front of me looked exactly like Alan. The only differences were the stitches from the coroner, when they pieced him back together after the accident. Images of that night began to race through my head as I remembered the last time I saw Alan. He was being chased by Joseph and ran out onto the highway. I was able to stop in time, but the big eighteen-wheeler next to me couldn't. With screeching tires , the big truck slammed into Shoe, dragging him behind.

I shook the visions from my mind and stared at Shoe. Now I had a chance to really have a look at him, I noticed his eyes were glossed over. The pupils were barely able to be seen. Just by looking at him I could tell the lights were on, but nobody was home. There was no way the monstrosity standing in front of me was Alan. I was there when he was hit by the truck. I saw his body or what was left of it. I went to his funeral. I've mourned him for the last few months. It couldn't be Shoe.

I glanced over at Selene and saw she had the same shocked expression as I did. Then she looked at me and yelled, "Run, Jack! I'll keep it busy long enough for you to get out of here!"

As if the corpse understood what Selene said, it lunged for me. I was on the other side of the bed, so it gave me the opportunity I needed to put Selene between me and it. I made a dash for the door and Alan tried to stop me, but Selene intercepted him. With a powerful kick, the were-panther sent Alan flying. With a bone breaking "CRUNCH," the corpse slammed into the wall and slumped to the floor. Selene took the opportunity to follow me down the stairs and out the front door.

"Come on, Jack!" Selene yelled as she grabbed the spare key from under the car. She unlocked the doors and got in.

"Get in!" Selene yelled again as the car started. "Hurry, it's not going to take it long to recover!"

I hurried to the passenger side of the car and opened the door, when Alan burst from the house. He looked at me just before I got in and I swore he smiled. It could have been a figment of my imagination or just the shadows across his face, but I could have sworn the corpse smiled at me.

Selene peeled out and a moment later Alan was an image in the rear view mirror. He shambled after us for a while, but once we were a ways off, he stopped.

"What was that?" I asked Selene once I was sure Alan was no longer pursuing us. "I know who it looked like, but was it really him or some sort of doppelganger?"

"That was a zombie," Selene replied and I just stared open mouthed at her. "I could smell the flesh rotting off his bones. Someone powerful must have cast a spell on his grave, animating his corpse. Apparently, somewhere down the line you pissed off a warlock and he thought it would be funny to send the reanimated corpse of your friend after you."

"I wonder if this has anything to do with Sarah," I said, remembering the night when we fought Nathaniel. "Maybe she was in some kind of coven and now they want revenge for her death."

"That could be," Selene said as she turned onto the street which led to La Luna. "But the first thing we must do is find some clothes to wear and get your wounds checked out."

"I'm alright," I said as I looked at the cuts on my arm. "None of the scratches are deep. No need for stitches this time."

"I'm not worried about how deep the cuts are," Selene said and with the tone in her voice I was starting to feel a little worried. "I'm more concerned about the diseases the corpse may have been carrying. I've heard tales of people dying after being attacked by a zombie. I've also heard of people turning into one if they get bit."

Once we arrived at La Luna Selene went to the phone and called Xylon. As soon as he answered I heard her say, "Xylon, Jack was attacked by a zombie. How fast can you make it to La Luna?"

There was silence for a moment, then I heard Selene say, "All right, we'll see you in half an hour. Thanks a lot, Xylon, and sorry for waking you."

As soon as Selene hung up I followed her down stairs. We always keep a spare change of clothes here just in case an emergency like this ever happened. Since neither of us were wearing much at the moment, we figured it would be better to switch into something a little less comfortable before Xylon arrived.

Like clockwork, a half hour later, Xylon arrived. As soon as he walked into the room he looked at me and said, "Hop up on the table over here and let me see your arm."

Xylon was thin and muscular, which seemed to be the normal build for a were-panther. He had wavy, shoulder length black hair and green eyes. He has saved mine and Selene's lives several times and has proved to be a very good friend.

I sat on the table and Xylon started examining my arm. He began cleaning and sterilizing my wounds, even though Selene and I already did it before he arrived. Once he was finished I saw him grab a needle and that was when my heart began to race.

"What do you need that thing for?" I asked, not liking the fact I was about to get another shot. Especially since I didn't think I was going to need another. "The cuts aren't deep enough for stitches."

"Don't be such a baby," Xylon said as he walked over to me and without warning he stuck the needle in my arm. Needless to say, I flinched. "It's an antibiotic, not a pain killer. With all the shots and stitches you've gotten over the last few months, one would figure you would be used to them by now."

"It's psychological," I said as I watched Xylon swab my arm with the alcohol covered cotton ball. "Some people are scared of heights, which is called vertigo. Others of enclosed places, which is claustrophobic. For me it's the fear of needles, which stands for, keep that damn thing away from me. I was held down and forced to get one as a kid and ever since then I have been terrified of them."

Xylon just looked at me for a moment, then shook his head and said, "What a big baby. How are you feeling, anyway?"

"Fine," I replied as I flexed my arm. "It doesn't even hurt."

"That's because of the pain killers the paramedics gave you for the stitches in your hand," Xylon said, which made sense. It also explains why I didn't feel the zombie ripping at my arm. "Believe me, once they wear off, you're going to be in pain. Every time you grab something the stitches will remind you of how much pain you're in."

"So, Doc, how is he?" Selene asked with a worried tone to her voice.

"We'll know more tomorrow," Xylon replied, which didn't help any. "He might be a little sick to the stomach tomorrow, but that's just a side effect to the antibiotics. I didn't see and sign of infection, which is a good thing. We'll just have to wait until tomorrow to find out more."

By the time Xylon finished bandaging up my arm it was already after four in the morning. Xylon had to be back here at nine for his shift and I had to be at Aces Pizza by eleven for mine. Something told me we weren't going to get any more sleep tonight.

While Xylon was patching me up, Selene had the rest of her Pride secure our house and make sure Zombie Shoe wasn't still lurking around. Once they gave us the "thumbs up" we headed back home.

There must have been some kind of sleep aid in the antibiotic Xylon gave me, because I felt very drowsy after we got home. I went up to our room and laid down. The last thing I remembered thinking about before I fell to sleep was going to Alan's grave in the morning and having a look. If it was truly him who attacked me, his grave would have been disturbed.

Chapter Five

I woke the next morning around ten-o-clock. Xylon was true to his word; I felt very sick to my stomach and just barely made it to the bathroom in time. Once I was finished reintroducing myself to last night's dinner, I noticed some blood in my vomit. I really hope it had nothing to do with the attack last night. I felt horrible; so bad I decided to call off work.

I went back to my room to get my phone, but once I reached it, I had a call. I answered it without looking to see who it was, which was something I always try to avoid doing. Feeling like I do, there wasn't many people I wanted to talk to. This time was an exception. As soon as I answered the phone I heard Agent Jacopo say, "Jack, I heard you and Selene were attacked by some kids last night. Was it something our department should look into, or was it just some punks?"

"They were messengers from the Council," I replied and I swore I could feel Agent Jacopo's excitement emanating over the phone. "They stopped by to invite Tyrone, Selene, and myself to a meeting. We refused and things got rough."

"Tyrone was there?" Agent Jacopo asked and the feeling of excitement doubled. "Did you find out where he is hiding Katrina?"

"No, but I know where Katrina's going to be," I replied and I started to feel really sick so I sat down on my bed. After a moment the sickness subsided and I was able to continue. "I have a meeting with her tonight."

"Where and when?" Agent Jacopo asked and this time I could hear the excitement in his voice. "I'll meet you there as back-up."

"After dark at the Rosemont Cemetery," I replied as the sickness in my stomach began to flare up again. "The same place I killed Boris."

"Alright, I'll see you there," Agent Jacopo said, then there was a click as he hung up. I wanted to tell him about the zombie, but I was extremely sick and all I wanted to do was sleep. I'm afraid the second part of my story from last night was going to have to wait.

As soon as I hung up with Agent Jacopo I called Aces Pizza. I felt horrible and didn't want to run around town for the next eight hours. I decided it would be best if I just called off, not to mention I still had to check out Alan's grave.

The phone rang three times before Danny answered, which meant they were busy. "Thanks for calling Aces Pizza, this is Danny, can I help you?"

"Hey, Danny," I replied after he finished. "It's Jack."

"Daaack," Danny said, which was the nickname he had for me. "How's it going?"

"I feel like crap," I replied, purposely sounding more pathetic than I actually was. "Is Tom there?"

"Yeah," Danny replied. "Hold on for a second. Let me get him for you."

Like I mentioned earlier, Tom is willing to work with his employees. If you were sick and needed a day off to recuperate, it was usually easy to get, usually.

Over the years I've worked for Tom we became good friends. So good I decided to let him in on my little secret. That secret changed his life forever. The supernatural does exist.

A couple months ago his family was being targeted by a pack of werewolves. Tom came to me for help and with the aid of my supernatural resources, we met the werewolves in battle. During one of our battles Tom was bitten and during the next full moon he transformed into a werewolf.

An old werewolf, named Thomas, helped us fight the werewolves, and when the fighting was over he took Tom as a pupil. Thomas showed him how to control the change and master the beast inside. Over the last couple months Tom has done well, but on the night of a full moon he must still be restrained. Silver chains are used to do this. Tom is shackled to a wall until morning. At that time he is released until the next full moon, where he will be chained again. The reason for this is if Tom should ever break his bonds, he will kill anyone it sees, even if they are friend or family.

There was silence as I was put on hold, then a couple moments later Tom came on the line. "What's up, Jack? Please, don't tell me you're sick. I already had to call Robert in to help deliver."

I explained everything which happened last night. Tom wasn't shocked to hear about the whole vampire incident. We've been expecting the Vampire Council for a couple months, but the news about Zombie Shoe threw him for a loop. Alan was also Tom's friend and the thought of him coming back as a zombie was heartbreaking and disturbing.

Tom was sympathetic of the fact I wasn't feeling well. He told me to take it easy today and get some rest. Which was exactly what I had plans of doing. I went back to bed and within moments I was asleep.

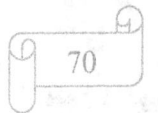

Chapter Six

I woke later in the day and felt much better. My stomach was still a little queasy, but nothing like it was earlier. I sat up in bed and saw it was going on five-o-clock in the afternoon. The sun was starting to set, so I figured I had better get to the cemetery before it was too late.

Selene wasn't in bed, so I figured she left earlier; most likely at La Luna. When I was up earlier I didn't even notice if she was still here or not. Then again, with how I was feeling I probably wouldn't even notice if Zombie Shoe was sitting next to me.

After sitting in bed for a few moments I decided to get up. As soon as I was dressed, I loaded my .380 with wood tipped bullets and my shotgun with shells full of wood chips. I put on my trench and fastened the shotgun inside, then I headed out. Even though I was hungry I skipped eating. I didn't want to take the chance of having to vomit again.

I drove to the Rosemont Cemetery and parked in the parking lot which was closes to where Alan was buried . I got out and walked the short distance to his grave. Once I got there I could tell instantly the ground had been disturbed. The thing in my bedroom last night was Alan's corpse. Right there and then I became sick to my stomach again. Just the thought of Shoe's body being used as a zombie made me sick. I hurried back to my car, not able to be near the grave any longer.

Once the sickness to my stomach subsided, I just sat there in my car. Memories of Alan raced through my mind. I missed him, and no matter how much I tried not to, I wept. A few moments later I was a total mess. My eyes were red and puffy and my nose was runny. I grabbed a napkin from the glove box and cleaned myself. When I was finished my phone rang. I looked to see who it was and saw Selene's number on the screen. As soon as I answered the phone she said, "Jack, where are you? I went to Aces after I left La Luna and Tom said you called off sick."

"I'm at the Rosemont Cemetery," I said as I started my car. "I needed to see for sure if it was Shoe who attacked me last night."

"I think I already know the answer to this, but was it?" Selene asked and I could tell from her voice, for my sake, she hoped it wasn't.

"Yes, it was him," I replied and I heard

Selene let out a slight sigh. "What did you mean by you already knew the answer?"

"I talked to my Pride this morning and they told me there wasn't any sign of a break-in," Selene replied and I wasn't sure what she meant. There had to have been a forceful entry for the zombie to get into our house. "The only other means for the zombie to enter without force was magic."

"What do you mean?" I asked, not knowing much about magic and the Occult. "How would magic get a zombie into our house?"

"Teleportation," Selene replied and the only thing I thought was, tele…what? "If killing Sarah is the reason why a warlock is after you, then we pissed off a really powerful one. From what I've heard , zombie raising and teleportation are not novice spells. Only the most powerful warlocks and witches have the ability to learn them."

"Great," I said, frustrated. Needless to say, things were getting out of hand. "I already have very powerful vampires after me and I'm sure the werewolf community aren't fans. One of my friends was brought back as a flesh eating zombie, and I'm the main course. Now, a powerful warlock wants to join in. What's next? Toe biting brownies and nose nipping pixies? I can't take this anymore."

By the time I was finished ranting, Selene was laughing. I guess on her end I sounded like a rave, striking lunatic. While Selene was getting herself under control, I noticed the sun was starting to set. I looked at the time and saw it was a little past six-o-clock. We had less than an hour before it was dark.

"You had better get over here," I said once Selene was finished laughing. "It's going to be dark soon"

"I'm on my way," Selene said, and I heard her car start in the background. "Just stay in the car until I get there. We don't need you rousing the anger of some kind of crypt fiend."

"Ha ha, real funny," I said and Selene just laughed. "By the way, you may want to bring along some back up. We don't know if Katrina is planning something behind our backs. Tabitha and Zack will be there. Hopefully, Jean Luke will also decide to show up with his coven."

"Xylon and Cleo are working a shift at La Luna tonight," Selene said and I knew that just cut our forces by half. "I'll give Kalinin and Zeana a call. They should be there by dark."

"Sounds great," I said, but I knew without Xylon and Cleo we would be shorthanded. "I'll give Shaun a call and see if he has any plans tonight. I'm sure he would like the opportunity to piss off Katrina again."

"Sounds good to me. I'll see you soon," Selene said and then we hung up. As soon as I hung up I gave Shaun a call. The phone rang three times, then I heard him pick up.

"Hello," Shaun said and he sounded excited and out of breath.

Over the past few months Shaun has become a real good friend. He saved my life numerous times , but he was there with me the night it all started. If it wasn't for him I would have been killed on a dark stretch of road. The police would have found my car, either that night or in the morning. They would have followed the drag marks out into the prairie and found my body, drained of all its blood and maybe even mauled by an animal. Nothing over the last few months would ever have happened. I would never have met Selene. Alan and Detective Oswald may have lived a long and happy life. Sometimes I wish Shaun wasn't there that night. Maybe things would have been better. I know it would have been for Shoe.

"Shaun, its Jack," I said as I wondered why

he was worked up. "What's going on? You sound out of breath."

"I just found out where Katrina's going to be tonight," Shaun replied and that explained the excitement. "My informant overheard Zack and Jean Luke talking about Katrina. He said he didn't hear much of the conversation, just that Katrina is having a meeting tonight with someone to discuss the matter about the Vampire Council, who is also in town. Did you know that?"

"I did," I replied, thinking to myself I should have told Shaun earlier about what happened. "I also know who Katrina's meeting."

"Who and how the heck did you find out about all of this?" Shaun asked and if he didn't sound so irritated I would have laughed.

"Katrina's meeting with me," I replied and for a moment there was silence on the other end of the line. Then I heard Shaun yell, "WHAT!? Why didn't you tell me!?"

"That's what I'm calling right now to do," I replied and the yelling on the other side stopped. I explained everything that happened to Shaun and he understood why I didn't contact him right away, at least I hope he does.

"I better get a move on then," Shaun said, then I heard him drop something in the background. "CRAP! That could have been bad. All right, it will be dark in less than an hour. Like all the other times, I'll be there. You won't see me, but I'll be there."

There was a click then the line went dead. I put the phone back in my pocket, then for the first time since I don't remember when, I prayed. I always believed in God, I just never thought myself worthy of prayer. I have sinned much over the years, to the point I was even embarrassed to ask for forgiveness. No matter how much I didn't deserve forgiveness, my friends needed all the help they could get, so I prayed. Straight from my heart I poured out my most sincere apology for all the wrong deeds I have done. I begged for forgiveness, but most of all I asked for help. I wasn't sure if my prayer was heard, but I felt better afterwards. Kind of like a weight was lifted from my shoulders.

Once I was finished I headed to where I was supposed to meet Katrina. I round a bend and standing on the side of the road, next to a garden of roses, was a little girl. She had blond hair, which she kept in piggy tails, and blue eyes. The little girl couldn't be any older than nine, but I didn't see her parents anywhere. The girl stared at me as I drove by. I looked everywhere, but she was alone. Every one of my senses screamed something wasn't right about this, but I couldn't help myself. I stopped my car and put it in reverse. I pulled up next to the little girl and asked, "Are you alright, little girl?"

She nodded with a smile. At first I expected to sense supernatural a moment before she sprouted fangs and attacked me, but there was nothing. For all I could tell, she was nothing more than a little girl.

"Are you alone?" I asked the little girl and she shook her head. "Where's your mommy and daddy?"

"I don't have a mommy," the little girl replied as she stared at me with big blue eyes.

"Where's your daddy?" I asked as I looked around, but no one could be seen. "Is he here?"

The little girl nodded again. I looked around once more and didn't see anyone, so I asked, "Where?"

"My father is in heaven," The little girl replied and at that moment I felt bad for her. She didn't have a mom and her father was dead.

"Who are you here with?" I asked and I still couldn't see anyone besides the girl.

"My father," the little girl replied and things were starting to make sense. She must have come here to visit her father's grave.

"Does anyone besides your father know you are here?" I asked and she nodded. "Do you live nearby?"

The little girl nodded again, then she asked, "Why are you here?"

"I came to check on a friend," I replied and she smiled.

"Did you have a good visit?" The little girl asked and I shook my head. "Why?"

"Because he wasn't home," I replied and the little girl got a confused look on her face. "It's getting dark, do you need a ride home?"

The little girl shook her head and replied, "No. I know the way."

"Alright," I said as I smiled at the little girl. "You had better get home while there's still enough light to see."

The little girl giggled, then she turned and walked away. I was about to drive away when she turned back towards me and waved, then she smiled and said, "My father likes you. He says you're a good person."

With those words the little girl giggled and ran off. I watched her until she disappeared behind a group of trees, then I continued on the way to my meeting with Katrina.

Chapter Seven

I arrived at the location where I was supposed to meet Katrina just before dark. Off in the distance I saw car lights and figured it was Selene. I was sure Agent Jacopo and Shaun were already here, but they were being all covert. While I'm standing down here with the vampires, their off, safely in the distance with high powered rifles.

As I watched the car lights wind around the cemetery I saw another set of lights enter through the main gate. I wasn't sure who that was. I didn't think it would be Katrina. She would be more covert style like Shaun and Agent Jacopo, especially with the Vampire Council looking for her.

As the first car pulled up I saw I was right, it was Selene. She parked her car next to mine and got out. Selene walked over and hugged me, while nuzzling her head under my chin. I kissed her gently on the forehead and asked, "Who's in the second car?"

"Kalinin and Zeana," Selene replied, and it made sense. She did say she was going to tell them to meet us here.

Kalinin was tall, standing around six feet four inches. He has long, wavy black hair and is extremely muscular. When I first met him I swore he could take first place in a body building competition, and today I still do.

Zeana has long, chestnut brown hair and a slim figure. Not overly skinny, but still not undesirable. She wasn't as attractive as Selene, but she had very striking features that would make her stand out among other woman.

Together, we watched as the car wound around the many bends of the cemetery, until it finally pulled up next to our cars. Kalinin and Zeana got out and walked up to us. Zeana hugged Selene, then me. After that, Kalinin took his turn with the hugging, but when it came to hugging me he just held out his hand and I happily shook it. I was actually kind of shocked. Were-panthers are big on emotion, but I'm not into hugging other guys. I guess Selene must have told Kalinin I was uncomfortable with it.

"How touching," a familiar voice said from behind us. "It's a good thing were just here to talk or all of you would be dead by now."

I sensed supernatural as I turned to see Katrina and five other people standing behind us.

She stared at me with her green eyes. Her long red hair was draped over her shoulders. Katrina wore a black evening dress slit up to the hip on the left side, exposing a generous amount of leg. A glossy black leather belt and red high heel shoes completed her outfit.

Besides Katrina I recognized four of the other five vampires. The first one was Tyrone, and even though I never got their names, I knew the other three from our battle with the werewolves. There was two males and one female. They disappeared after Katrina was taken into custody. Even Jean Luke couldn't find them.

All three of the vampires from the werewolf battle looked to be in their twenties. One of the men had short black hair and he was dressed in a black suit with a red tie. He looked a lot like one of Katrina's servants who was killed a few months ago by Nathaniel. His name was Sam.

The other male vampire had brown hair that looked like he just came out of a hurricane. He wore blue jeans and a t-shirt. The female vampire was very beautiful and petite. She had long black hair and was dressed in a black t-shirt and leather pants. The t-shirt had a logo of a modern day rock band on it.

The new vampire has dark skin, but not as

dark as Tyrone. He also looked to be in his twenties and had short, nappy, black hair. He wore a t-shirt and blue jeans, but he also wore lots of jewelry. I guess today's generation would call that "bling." To me he just looked like a want to be gang bang rapper. He just stared at us with a smirk on his face and he laughed at Katrina's comment. I could already tell this guy was going to be trouble.

"I'm amazed, Jack," Katrina said with a smile that showed off her fangs. "You only brought three other people with you. I figured you would have an army here, like you did when we fought the werewolves."

"My indication was we were just here to talk," I said as I ignored Katrina's new flunky and kept my concentration on her. "The only reason why Kalinin and Zeana are here is just in case the four vampires from last night show up again"

"Come on, Jack," Katrina said as she looked past me and out into the darkness around us. "Are you trying to tell me, Shaun isn't out there somewhere with his rifle pointed at my heart?"

"Maybe he is," I said and I couldn't hide my smile. "I couldn't tell you, but if he is, then it only a precaution."

"Even with your homie out there," the new

vampire said with a sadistic smile. "You and a hand full of cats wouldn't stand a chance against us if we wanted to cap ya."

I was about to say something to him, but Tyrone beat me to it. "Hey, Dallas. How many masters have you killed?"

"None, but what's that got to do with anything?" Dallas asked as he glanced at Tyrone, then back to me.

"Jack's killed two in the last few months," Tyrone replied and the smile faded from Dallas' face. "Not to mention the leader of a werewolf pack. So why don't you just shut up before you get your ass staked."

Dallas didn't like Tyrone's comment, but he chose to remain quiet. Personally, I thought it was a good idea. I've been taking Kiki's crap for the last few months, the last thing I need is too take attitude from this punk.

"Are we going to do this or not?" I asked and I couldn't hide the irritation in my voice. My stomach was starting to hurt again and all I wanted to do is go home and lay down.

"Fine," Katrina replied as she got a serious look on her face. "Tyrone told me about what happened last night with the Council. They haven't been able to find me so their coming after you."

"Why the heck do they care about me?" I asked and I was getting severely tired of always getting caught up in all the vampire drama. "I don't know where you're spending your nights or even how to contact you. Not to mention, if they want me dead, all they have to do is kill you."

"They're the Vampire Council, Jack," Katrina replied and her voice had a nervous tone to it. "First of all, not only have you killed a large amount of vampires over the last three months, but two of them were masters. Also, if they had you, they could easily find me. They have warlocks that can do location spells by using the bond we share with each other."

Selene and I just stared at each other. This may have just explained who brought Alan back as a zombie. Now, I had my own reason to find the Council, or at least the warlock who is making my life hell.

"I thought all the Vampire Council wanted to do was talk to you?" I asked even though I knew it would be a one sided talk and Katrina wouldn't be the one doing the talking.

"They're here to put me on trial for the two

masters you killed. Are you willing to stake your life on them just wanting to talk?" Katrina asked and this time I got quiet. "That's what I thought."

"So what do you suppose we should do then?" I asked and I knew I wasn't going to like her answer.

"You could always enlist the help of Jean Luke and his coven," Katrina replied and I was sure he would help us with the Council if push came to shove, but I really didn't want to get his coven involved. I didn't want to put their lives at stake, no pun intended. "Selene can also bring her Pride."

"Don't bring my Pride into this," Selene said and I could hear the anger in her voice. "I could care less what happens to you and your coven. Were only here to back up Jack."

"What do you think will happen to Jack if the Council gets their claws on me?" Katrina asked and once again she had us speechless. "We need to find out where they are, gather our forces and strike before they have time to act."

"That would be an excellent plan, Katrina," an unfamiliar voice said from the shadows and I immediately sensed another supernatural presence. "Except for the fact we now know of it."

I saw Katrina's pale skin become even paler. I had no idea who the voice belonged too, but apparently she did. Everyone turned in the direction where we heard it and out of the shadows walked a man with neatly groomed black hair and mustache. He stood close to six feet tall and wore a very expensive suit.

Behind him, still lurking in the shadows was another man. I couldn't tell much about his features because the shadows obscured them. I did notice he was just under six feet tall and also wore a very nice suit. Another thing I noticed, which was very annoying, he was staring at me. The whole time he stood there, his eyes were completely on me.

The man who spoke approached us and said, "Hello, Katrina. It's been a while."

"Yes it has, Antonio," Katrina said and for the first time ever, I heard true fear in her voice. "Is the rest of the Vampire Council with you?"

"They are not aware of this meeting," Antonio replied as he eyed every one of us. "They will be at your trial. I wished to speak with you before then, but first of all let me introduce my human servant, Brian Richards."

The man stepped forward from the shadows, the whole time staring at me with his dark blue eyes. As I looked into those eyes I saw hatred. I was sure if he had the opportunity, this man would try to kill me. He looked close to fifty and had a well-trimmed beard. Like his hair, the beard was more gray than black.

"What is it you wish to talk about?" Katrina asked and there was a slight quiver to her voice.

"That matter can wait," Antonio replied as a smile snaked across his face. "Please, continue with your meeting. Don't let my presence here interfere."

"If you don't mind me asking, my lord," Katrina said and it was nice seeing her grovel. "No one knew of this meeting besides us, how did you know where to find us?"

"As soon as Nathaniel contacted me a couple months ago I sent my spies to investigate what was going on down here," Antonio replied as the smile on his face grew wider. "Once Boris was killed we knew a takeover was in progress. Then Nathaniel and his son was killed shortly after, all three by your human servant and his pussy cat. I didn't believe it could be done by a human servant at first, but my spies assured me there was something special about yours. I had to see this for my own eyes, so at once the Council gathered. We arrived two nights ago and once I had a chance to debrief my spies I sent David to find you. His mission was simple, find out just how powerful this Jack is. The results he brought back were very disappointing."

"Wait a second," I said as I looked at Antonio. "This is the Antonio Vesuvius from the Vampire Council?"

"I am," Antonio replied and the words slithered from his lips like poison. "And you're Jack Holladay. The wayward human servant of Katrina De' Luce. I have heard much about you, Jack, and I don't like any of it."

"Feelings are mutual," I said and I saw Antonio's eyes glow red for a second. "And what's the story with your human servant? Why can't he take his eyes off me?

"I'll show you why," Brian said and there was hatred in his voice. He took a step towards me, but Antonio stopped him.

"Now is not the time, my friend," Antonio said and for the first time since they arrived, Brian took his eyes off me and stared at Antonio. "You will soon have your revenge."

Brian's body trembled with rage, but he did what his master said. His eyes were still on me the whole time and it made me wonder what I did to make him want revenge.

"That's enough, Jack," Katrina said before I could say anything else to tick off Brian or his master. "The Council came all this way to see me, and now they are here. They will be treated with the respect they deserve."

"So now I deserve respect," Antonio said and he spat the words out when he did. "A moment ago you were making plans to destroy us."

I started to wonder if Agent Jacopo was here or not. If he was then why hasn't he tried to take revenge for his partner's murder? I looked out into the darkness, but couldn't see any movement. If Agent Jacopo was here, then he is showing a great deal of restraint.

"Am I boring you , Jack?" Antonio asked, drawing my attention away from my surroundings and back to him. "Or don't you see the severity you and Katrina are in?"

"Actually, I'm just trying to figure out why your still alive," I replied and this time I must have really hit a nerve, because not only did Antonio's eyes glow, his fist clenched as well.

It took Antonio a moment to compose himself, but once he did he smiled at me and said, "From your remark, I'm sure your referring to Agent Jacopo and the other snipers you had creeping around the cemetery. Yes, Jack, I did know about them. It wasn't hard to spot them when we arrived. Especially, since one of them was my spy."

At that time Antonio signaled to someone out in the darkness and a moment later the cemetery was full of movement. From all around us I sensed supernatural as vampires came out of hiding. They quietly approached us and with them were several humans.

When they were close enough for me to make out detail, I saw there were six humans and at least ten vampires. I recognized four of the vampires as David and his three flunkies and two of the humans as, Agent Jacopo and Shaun. The other humans wore suits like Agent Jacopo, so I figured they were F.B.I.P.A. agents. The vampires carried high powered rifles, which I figured were confiscated from the humans. The only human who still had a rifle was Agent Jacopo. My jaw dropped when I saw this. His story was so convincing I would never have guessed him as a spy. Then again, if I did he wouldn't have been a very good one.

When the group entered our meeting area Antonio said, "Are you surprised, Jack? To find out one of your friends was actually my spy."

"I have to admit, it was a shock," I replied as my hand slowly crept towards the .380 I had holstered on my hip. "So Agent Jacopo, is that your real name or were you just a mole Antonio placed in the F.B.I.P.A.?"

"First of all we need to get rid of that," Agent Jacopo said as he reached over and relieved me of my handgun. "You're a horrible shot, Jack, but at this range I don't think even you can miss. He also carries a shotgun in his trench."

David opened my trench and unstrapped my shotgun. He took it out and tossed it to Marko. The vampire smiled at me as he caught it.

"Everything I told you was real, Jack," Agent Jacopo replied as he took the clip out of my gun. "Antonio did kill my partner and he almost killed me , but it wasn't the arrival of my backup that saved me. I would have been dead by then if I didn't make a deal with Antonio. I would cover up disappearances when he or one of Antonio's minions decided to indulge themselves. I would also keep the F.B.I. one step behind his operations. If I did this he would spare my life. When I became a member of the F.B.I.P.A. it made things even easier for me. I was given my own team and tonight they will be given the same choice I was given. Join us or die."

Agent Jacopo looked at the first of his agents. He was older than the rest of the squad, I would say in his forties. His black hair was beginning to recede and he had a good deal of grey. The agent stared at Jacopo with cold eyes, then he said, "I guess this is when we choose to become a slave or the meal for a vampire. Well, sir. I would say this with deep respect, but you lost that when you handed us over to a bunch of bloodsuckers. I don't know if I speak for the others, but kiss my a…"

Before the agent could finish his sentence David snapped his neck. His lifeless body fell to the ground, then Agent Jacopo looked at another agent and said, "Next."

The agent looked down at the corpse of his team member, then to Jacopo. Everyone could see the fear in his eyes, the vampires could smell it and they took pleasure in it. I looked at Katrina and even though she was scared, she also got off on the scent. The only vampire present who didn't look like he was in a stage of bliss was Tyrone. I could tell the big vampire was appalled by this cleansing. He looked away and our eyes met. At that time I could tell, no matter how much he loved Katrina for saving his life, he was ashamed of what he became.

Jacopo stared at the agent and the man whimpered as his body began to shake. He lost control of his bodily functions, then David said, "To late," as he snapped the agent's neck.

"Enough of this," Brian said as he stared at me. "I will have my revenge, now!"

Brian stepped forward and raised his hands towards the last two agents. Lightning shot from his finger tips and struck them. The two men fell to the ground in pain as their bodies convulsed. Their screams were so loud my head began to hurt. I saw the agent's skin begin to smolder and bubble, then Brian stopped his attack and the two men were dead. The night air was filled with burned flesh. The smell was sickening and my stomach started to turn. I was sick enough the way it was, but this pushed me over the edge and I retched.

"Look, Brian," Antonio said as he pointed to my vomit. "Your curse has begun to take effect."

I looked down and saw only blood. I haven't eaten anything today so there was nothing in my stomach. Selene came to my side, but before she could touch me, Brian yelled, "Get away from him, you bitch!"

Once again, lightning shot from Brian's fingertips and as they hit Selene, she began to scream. I smelt her flesh begin to burn and I was too weak to do anything.

Kalinin and Zeana leaped towards Brian, transforming into their hybrid forms as they did. Kalinin was caught in mid-air by David and Marko. The were-panther was pulled to the ground. Claws and fists struck him until he no longer moved, but even then the vampires didn't stop.

Zeana got within striking distance of Brian, but it was in vain. Antonio was waiting for her. The vampire back handed the were-panther a moment before her claws struck home. Zeana flew out of the clearing and slammed into a tree. There was a sickening crack as she hit, then her body slumped to the ground.

Seeing the were-panthers were out of the fight, Shaun tried to take his rifle from a vampire's grasp. I guess he was hoping to take the bloodsucker by surprise, because Shaun was nowhere near strong enough to wrestle it from him. The vampire wretched the rifle from Shaun's grasp and all my friend got from his efforts was the rifle's butt to his face.

Selene continued to scream as I slowly got to my feet. I didn't have any weapons and my body felt like someone put me through a meat grinder, but I had to do something to save her. I took a staggering step towards Brian, but before I could take another a vampire grabbed me. I stared at the warlock and with tears in my eyes I asked, "Please stop. Why are you doing this? What did we do to make you need revenge?"

"YOU KILLED SARAH!" Brian screamed as Selene's charred form ceased to move. "You killed my daughter, my baby girl. Since you took someone so precious from me, I will do the same to you."

"Jack and Selene didn't kill Sarah," Shaun said as he got back to his feet. "I did. I shot her from across the room."

"YOU!!" Brian screamed as he redirected the lightning towards Shaun. "I will kill you, but not fast. You will suffer a long time before I finally decide to take my revenge."

Once the lightning hit Shaun, he fell to the ground in pain. At first he didn't cry out, but everyone has their threshold. First, Brian concentrated the full force of the lightning on Shaun's foot. His cowboy boot burst into flames, igniting his jeans in the process. Shaun tried to slap out the fire, but every time he tried, Brian redirected the lightning at Shaun's chest, flooring him from the pain.

Being human, Shaun wasn't going to be able to withstand the torture much longer. I screamed at Brian to stop as I fought to break free of the vampire's grasp.

Tyrone looked down at Selene's smoldering body, then to Shaun. I'm not sure what made him do it, but with amazing speed the big vampire put his body between the lightning and Shaun. Tyrone grimaced in pain as he quickly patted out the fire, which was spreading up Shaun's leg.

"No, Tyrone!" Katrina yelled as the big vampire slowly staggered to his feet as the lightning burned and bubbled his flesh. "Stop, they will kill you!"

Tyrone fought the lightning as he took one agonizing step after another towards Brian. By the time the big vampire reached the warlock his body was badly charred and blistered. Blood and puss streamed down from his many wounds. Tyrone's eyes exploded in their sockets as the lightning struck his head, but even that didn't stop him. Tyrone raised his big, clawed hand to strike down Brian, but before he could, Antonio ripped out the big vampire's throat. Tyrone staggered back a couple feet before he finally fell. He clenched at his throat as blood gushed out and even though I knew vampires didn't need to breathe, they could still bleed out.

I wanted to help Tyrone, but there was nothing I could do. Selene laid a couple feet from me and I didn't know if she was alive or dead. Shaun clenched his leg as he grimaced in pain. Zeana was barely moving and Kalinin's body was so ripped up, I don't even think his regeneration ability could heal him.

Brian continued to fry Tyrone as I caught movement out of the corner of my eye. A moment later Jean Luke crashed into Brian, canceling his spell as they both tumbled to the ground. Seeing his human servant in jeopardy, Antonio went to his aid.

A moment later a hand erupted from Marko's chest. The vampire stared at its still beating heart before crumbling to the ground and imploding into a little black marble. Where Marko once stood, was now Zack. His arm was covered with blood as he dropped Marko's disintegrating heart.

Zack picked up my shotgun and slammed the butt into David's face, then he tossed it to me while saying, "Catch, Jack."

The shotgun hit the ground at my feet as Zack traded punches with David. I tried again to break the vampire's grasp who held me, but I couldn't. Then I heard the sound of gunfire and the vampire's grasped loosened as it imploded into the little black marble. I looked around to see who shot the vampire and saw Jarvis, no more than thirty feet away. He had a rifle in hand and was targeting another vampire.

I picked up my shotgun, then went over to check on Selene. She was alive, but in bad shape. I could only hope her regeneration ability was strong enough to bring her back from this.

As I was checking on Selene I saw Agent Jacopo aim his rifle at Jean Luke. The master vampire had his attention on Antonio and Brian and didn't notice his impending doom. I pointed my shotgun at Agent Jacopo, but before I could pull the trigger, Tabitha arrived on the scene. In a blink of the eye she pulled the barrel of Jacopo's rifle. The weapon went off, but instead of hitting Jean Luke, the wood tipped bullet struck Antonio in the arm. The vampire hissed as he clenched the wound.

Jean Luke took the opportunity to regain control. With incredible speed he slashed at

Antonio with his claws, cutting deep across the vampire's chest and destroying his expensive suit.

I noticed Brian beginning to cast a spell at Jean Luke and since Tabitha had Agent Jacopo under control I took aim at the warlock. As Brian neared the end of his spell I pulled the trigger. Wood chips exploded from the barrel of my shotgun, hitting the warlock in several different places. Several chunks imbedded themselves deep within his skin. Brian screamed and lost concentration on his spell. The warlock stared at me as blood flowed from his left eye and many other wounds, but since he wasn't a vampire, the shot didn't kill him. It just hurt like hell.

A moment later Terrance and Kiki joined the battle, both of them attacked David's flunkies, since they came to help him against Zack. Things were looking up for us, but even with Jean Luke's reinforcements, we were still outnumbered. I looked over at Katrina, who was doing nothing more than watching the battle and yelled, "This is your chance, Katrina. Help us and we may survive this night."

At first I thought Katrina wasn't going to do anything, but then she and her minions joined the fight. Now we had the upper hand.

Jarvis took out another vampire and with the

help of Katrina's coven we were able to push back. Both of David's flunkies were torn to shreds by Terrance, Kiki, and Dallas, while David himself tried to hold his own against Zack.

Seeing his forces were being depleted, Antonio commanded the rest of his servants to flee. Brian said a word I didn't understand and a moment later he was gone. The rest of Antonio's minions disappeared into the night. Our forces gave pursuit, but it wasn't long before they came back. Every single surviving vampire of Antonio's was gone, but in their haste to survive, they left behind Agent Jacopo.

Tabitha had him in her grasp, and no matter how hard Agent Jacopo struggled, he couldn't break her hold. I just stared at him for a moment and when he noticed me, he looked away. We won the battle, but at a great cost.

I held Selene's hand, dreading the worst. I saw her eye flicker, then it opened. She was in horrible pain, but she was conscious. Slowly, I saw her wounds begin to heal, and hope filled me. Selene looked into my eyes and with cracked lips, she smiled.

As I held onto Selene's hand I heard a moan from a few feet away. I looked in that direction and saw Tyrone. The big vampire was lying in a pool of his own blood. I looked down at Selene and said, "I'm going to check on Tyrone."

Selene nodded and I laid her hand, gently, on her chest. Tyrone was face down, so I rolled him over. The big vampire gurgled as he spat up blood. I saw he had burns over ninety percent of his body. His eyes were gone and the wound in his throat wasn't healing fast enough.

Tyrone's hand went up and I took it in mine. Tears began to fill my eyes as I said, "Hold in there, Tyrone. We're going to get you some help."

Tyrone smiled when he heard my voice, then with his last breath he said, "Jacky b$_{oyyy}$…"

Tears streamed down my face as Tyrone's smile faded and his hand went limp. His body imploded into a little black marble. For a moment I didn't do anything. I just knelt next to the little black sphere and wept. Tyrone was my friend. One you don't come across very often and now he was gone. I wanted to kill Antonio and Brian, but they were long gone, so I turned my anger to the one I could.

"You son of a bitch," I said as I picked up Tyrone's marble and put it in my pocket. I got to my feet and stormed over to Agent Jacopo. I cocked my shotgun and pointed it at his head.

Agent Jacopo flinched and closed his eyes as the cold metal touched his temple. I stood there, my arms shaking with fury, but I never took a man's life in cold blood before . I knew if I crossed that threshold, there would never be any coming back. Everyone watched me as I made my decision, but before I could Selene fought through the pain to a sitting position and in a weak voice she said, "No, Jack. Stop. Don't go there. Don't turn into something you're not."

I looked at Selene and she held her arms out to me. Then I looked back at Agent Jacopo. He stared up at me, his eyes pleading for his life. I closed mine and gritted my teeth, then I lowered my weapon and walked over to Selene's embrace.

As I held Selene, Zack walked over to Agent Jacopo, pulled a handgun out of the agent's belt and put a clip into it. I recognized it as my .380. Zack chambered a bullet and said, "Tyrone was my friend and you took him away from me. Jack may not be able to venture into the dark side, but that's where I live."

With those words Zack put my .380 to Agent Jacopo's head and pulled the trigger. The impact from the bullet sent Jacopo staggering back a couple feet before his body crashed lifeless to the ground. Zack lowered the gun, walked over to me. He handed me the gun and said, "I think this is yours."

I took the handgun and put it back in its holster, then I heard Selene say, "How is Kalinin and Zeana?"

Terrance walked over to where Kalinin's body was, then looked over at me and shook his head. I feared the worst when I saw David and Marko beat the life out of him.

Selene burst into tears at the news of her friend's death. I looked over to where I saw Zeana land and saw Jean Luke checking on her. He knelt down and picked her up. Her arm went around the vampire's shoulder and she looked over at us. Zeana was still alive. Even though Selene cried for the loss of a friend, she smiled at the life of another. Jean Luke brought Zeana over to us and laid her down. Even though Selene was in horrible pain she hugged her friend.

Besides Tyrone, Katrina lost another of her minions. Besides Dallas I didn't know any of their names. All I know, it was the guy with the wind blown hair. Katrina said his name was John.

Jean Luke took care of Agent Jacopo's body. He assured me it would never be found, which made me happy since Zack used my gun to kill him. Jean Luke also made arrangements to have Kalinin's body delivered to Selene when she was ready to hold a funeral. Right now she needed time to heal and morn.

Thanks to Tyrone, Shaun will survive. His right foot was destroyed by Brian's lightning and he'll be bed ridden for a while, but at least he'll live.

Selene figured it was better if Shaun was cared for by Xylon. It would be hard to explain to the police how this happened to him. Shaun didn't care. He just wanted to get back into the fight as soon as possible.

Selene had me call Xylon and tell him what happened. He was grief stricken when he heard about Kalinin. Selene told me to make sure he had the medical room prepped for three and for once it wasn't for me.

Chapter Eight

Selene, Zeana, and Shaun arrived at La Luna about fifteen minutes before me. Jean Luke figured it would be better if he, Kiki, and Tabitha carried them there. They would get to La Luna faster by using their supernatural speed. Not only that, but if I got pulled over by the police on the way there, I wouldn't have to worry about explaining why I have two electrocuted and one beat up person in the car with me.

I asked what we were going to do about Selene and Zeana's cars, and Jean Luke had Zack and Terrance drive them to La Luna. Zack wanted to drive my car instead, but I forbid it. With him behind the wheel of my convertible Camaro, he was bound to get pulled over.

We asked Shaun what he wanted to do with his truck since no one knew where he parked it and he said, "Don't worry about it. It's safe where it is. If all else I'll just have Jarvis drive it home."

Once I arrived at La Luna I got out of my car as Zack and Terrance pulled up in the other cars. Zack got out of Selene's car and tossed me her keys.

"You should have let me drive your car," Zack said as Terrance walked over and handed me Zeana's keys. "All that power is being wasted on you. You barely broke the speed limit twice on the way here."

"Well, the idea was not to arouse the attention of the authorities," I said as I put the keys in my pocket. "Not to mention I wanted to get my car here in one piece."

"Let's get going, Zack," Terrance said as he gave the vampire a nudge. "Jean Luke wants us back at the mansion right away. Not to mention, I'm sure Jack wants to check in on Selene."

"Fine. Later's, Jack," Zack said, then with their supernatural speed they were instantly gone.

Once Zack and Terrance were gone I walked up to the front door and tried to open it, but it was locked. A moment later I sensed supernatural from the other side and heard a click. The door opened and I saw Cleo. Her eyes were red and puffy, and her mascara was streaked down her cheeks. As soon as Cleo saw me she wrapped her arms around me and cried. I picked up the young were-panther and carried her inside. After kicking the door shut I carried Cleo over to a chair and sat her down. Kalinin was a good friend of hers. Being part of

Selene's Pride meant they were practically family.

I knelt down next to Cleo and held her in my arms. I wanted to tell her things were going to be alright, that the pain will go away in time, but it really doesn't. You just learn to deal with it. I didn't know what to say to Cleo, so I just held her until she didn't have any more tears to cry.

Once the sobbing had stopped I cupped Cleo's chin in my hand and said, "I'm going to go downstairs and check on Selene. Are you going to be alright by yourself?"

"I'll come with you," Cleo replied as she stood from her seat. "I'm all out of tears, right now."

Together, Cleo and I went downstairs to the Pride's homemade medical room. We had everything down here a major hospital would have and Xylon knew how to use all of it.

As soon as we were downstairs I saw Selene lying on one of the beds. Next to her was Zeana and down a little ways was Shaun. Jean Luke and the rest of his coven had already left.

I walked over to Selene and took her hand in mine. She smiled at me and I was happy to see she already looked better than before. She was strapped up to an I.V. and a heart monitor. If I was reading the machine right it was saying her heart rate was strong.

"How are you doing?" I asked and I couldn't hide the concern in my voice if I wanted to.

"I'm feeling much better," Selene replied, wincing in pain as she adjusted her position. "Xylon gave me something to kick my regeneration into high gear. I should be fully healed in a day or so."

"She should be ready to go home tomorrow," Xylon said as he checked Selene's I.V. lines. "Now, what is this I hear about you vomiting blood?"

"My stomach has been upset since yesterday morning after being attacked by Zombie Shoe," I replied and I was a little worried about having to get another shot. "I'm fine, really. No need for needles, Doc."

"I would still like to check your vitals while I have you here," Xylon said and even though I didn't want him to, I figured it was probably best he did.

I agreed to the examination and Xylon had me hop up on the bed next to Zeana. As I sat there

I looked at the were-panther and asked, "How are you doing, Zeana?"

"I'm healing," Zeana replied and she still looked a little pale, but nowhere near as bad as Selene. "Xylon told me Antonio broke my spine. If it wasn't for my regeneration ability, I would have been crippled for the rest of my life."

"You're lucky the impact didn't break your neck," Xylon said as he came over to check on me. "Even your regeneration wouldn't have saved you from that. You're going to be bed ridden for the next two or three days the way it is."

Xylon checked my vitals, then my reflexes. He even went as far as take x-rays. Once he was finished he said, "Your heart rate is lower than what it should be and you have a slight temperature. Your lungs sound like there might be a little bit of liquid in them, but the thing that has me concerned most of all is the spots on your stomach. If you look at these x-rays of your stomach you can see them. It's not normal and I've never seen anything like it before. Are you sure you're feeling alright?"

"I guess so," I replied as I looked at the x-ray. "Besides the stomach ache I don't feel any different."

"I want you to spend the night here," Xylon said and since I didn't want to leave Selene, I had plans of doing so anyway. "I have some pills for you to take, then I want to monitor you over night and see how you feel in the morning."

I agreed and Xylon got the pills for me. While he was fetching the pills I looked over at Shaun and saw he was sleeping. His right leg was wrapped up, and from what I could see from where I was, his foot was amputated. After seeing how much damage it took, I wasn't surprised. I felt so bad for Shaun. He's been through so much over the years, but when you hunt the supernatural, things like this happening are to be expected. I just didn't know how it was going to affect Shaun's lifestyle as a vampire slayer.

A moment later Xylon returned with my pills. He told me they were very powerful and was probably going to knock me out for the night. He wasn't kidding. The last thing I remembered was watching Selene as she tried to rest, then nothing.

Chapter Nine

I woke the next morning and like before I made a mad dash to the bathroom. Luckily, the one at La Luna was closer to me than at home. There wasn't anything in my stomach since I haven't eaten for over a day, but when I vomited, my stomach was full of blood.

My body broke out in a cold sweat and my stomach was extremely upset, worse than yesterday. I felt extremely dizzy when I stood and was forced to lean against the wall to steady myself. Once I was able to walk I stumbled back out to my bed and laid down.

Xylon was looking at me when I left the bathroom. He was sitting on the side of one of the numerous beds in the room. He rubbed his eyes and with a yawn he said, "I could hear you all the way out here. Did you vomit blood again?"

"Yeah," I replied as I laid on the bed with my eyes closed. "I feel worse today than yesterday. I need to call Tom and let him know I won't be coming in."

"It's strange those pills I gave you last night didn't help your stomach any," Xylon said as he ran his fingers through his long, black hair. "I need to take another x-ray of your stomach."

"I wish we could do that from here," I said as I looked at Xylon. "I feel like crap and I really don't want to move."

"I'll get a wheel chair and give you a ride over to the x-ray room," Xylon said as he hopped off the bed and walked over to the nearest wheel chair. "I would let you rest, but I need to see if there are any changes to your stomach."

Xylon helped me into the chair, then he wheeled me into the x-ray room. I laid on the table, the whole time feeling like I was about to throw-up. The whole process took about ten minutes, then Xylon helped me back into the chair and out to my bed.

I laid in bed for about half an hour, then Xylon came out of the back room with the x-rays. He pulled up a chair and sat down next to me, then said, "I'm afraid your stomach has gotten worse. The red spots have gotten bigger and black splotches have begun to appear. It almost looks like your stomach is rotting away or you have a severely aggressive cancer."

"What does all of that mean?" I asked and I was starting to get a little worried.

"You're dying, Jack," Xylon said with a great deal of concern in his eyes. "At the rate the sickness is spreading, you may only have a week to live."

"I guess the curse Antoine was talking about is true," I said as I grimaced from the pain.

"What curse?" Xylon asked as he looked at me like I was losing my mind. "I only caught bits and pieces of what happened last night."

"Apparently, I was cursed by a warlock, who happen to be the father of Sarah," I replied and Xylon looked shocked. "Everything that's been happening to me and Selene lately has been part of his plot for revenge."

"Wait a second," Xylon said with a confused look. "You didn't kill Sarah. It was Shaun who shot her."

"Yeah, he found that out," I said as I glanced over at Shaun. "Which is the reason why his foot was destroyed. Brian was going to make Shaun suffer before avenging his daughter's death."

"What are you going to tell Selene?" Xylon asked as he looked at her.

"Nothing," I replied as I fought through another stomach pain. "She's been through a lot. I don't want to worry her."

"Worry me about what?" Selene asked as she rolled onto her side so she could look at me. "Does this have anything to do with the blood you threw-up?"

I didn't reply. I just looked at her, not wanting to worry her. Selene stared at me for a few moments, then when I wouldn't respond she looked at Xylon and said, "Tell me."

"I'm sorry, Jack, but Selene's my Alpha," Xylon said with a sigh. "Jack's been cursed by the warlock you ran into last night and unless something is done he is going to die within a week, maybe less if progresses faster."

"This isn't something you hide from me, Jack," Selene said and I couldn't tell if she was hurt or mad. "We need to do something about it today. Do we know anyone who has knowledge in magic?"

"I'm not sure," Xylon replied with a puzzled expression. "Over the years we've tried to keep

our association with spell casters at a minimum."

"I think I know of someone who could help us," I said and they both just looked at me. "I could have Robert talk to his Wicca friends, but if they come here it would reveal everything we try to keep hidden from the outside world. Another person we can talk to is my internet friend, Dennis Wiseman. He seems very knowledgeable about the supernatural. He may know about magic."

"Being knowledgeable is one thing," Xylon said as he ran his fingers through his hair and sighed. "But being able to cast the spell is another. Unless your friend can make a trip down here and cast the spell, his knowledge is useless to us."

"Then we have no choice," I said, understanding what Xylon meant. "I'll give Robert a call."

"It would save a lot of explaining if he could come to your house instead," Xylon said and I agreed, even though I didn't want to move. "Do you think you can make it to your car, Jack?"

"I'll help him," Selene said as she sat up. "Just let me get dressed and take a shower."

"Are you sure you're up to it?" I asked and Selene did look much better. Almost all of her blisters have healed and instead of charred flesh her skin looked more like she had a bad sunburn. I love the regenerative powers of were-panthers.

"I'm in better shape than you," Selene replied and I couldn't argue with that. "I should be completely healed by tomorrow morning."

I couldn't argue with Selene so I agreed. While she was in the shower I called Tom. I told him what happened last night and about our causalities. I also told him about the curse Brian put on me and how long I had to live. Tom kind of freaked out about the dying part. Needless to say, I didn't have to ask for the day off.

After I hung up with Tom, I called Robert. I didn't know what to tell him so I told him the truth. Well, at least the truth about being cursed by a warlock and having less than a week to live. Robert wasn't sure there was anything he could do. He had to talk to his Wicca friends and see if there was anything their coven could do.

After hanging up with Robert, Selene came out of the shower. With Xylon's help they got me out to Selene's car. I didn't like the idea of leaving my Camaro here. I'm sure it would be safe, but what if Zack stopped by. He would see it as a great opportunity to hotwire it and take it for a joyride. The thought unnerved me, but I was in no condition to drive.

On our way home, Robert called. He told me his friend was very interested in meeting me and could be at our house in a few hours. I agreed, wanting nothing more right now than to get rid of this curse.

Chapter Ten

Once we arrived at home Selene helped me inside. I'm sure we looked like a motley duo if anyone saw us. Instead of going to bed I laid on the couch in the living room, with a bucket at my side. I didn't see any reason to make Robert and his friends go all the way upstairs to see me.

A few hours after we got home there was a knock at the door. Selene answered it and invited everyone in. As soon as Robert saw me lying on the couch he said, "You look like hell, Jack."

Along with Robert there was three other men. Each of them looked to be Caucasian and in their early thirties.

Robert introduced he first man as John. He had brown eyes and short, black hair, which was parted to the side. He was well groomed and wore a dress shirt with slacks.

The second of the three men wore glasses. He had short, curly, black hair and blue eyes. He wore a striped polo and black dress pants. His name was Scott.

The last of the three men had long, wavy, blond hair, and a neatly trimmed goatee. He had blue eyes and thick eyebrows, but since they were blond, you really couldn't tell. A clean t-shirt and blue jeans were his choice in clothes. Robert said his name was Charles or Chuck for short.

I sat up to shake hands with Robert and the three men, but my stomach instantly turned and I almost vomited on John. Chuck laughed when he saw how quickly his friend stepped back, then said, "Well, that's one way to get a sample. Personally, I'd prefer to ask for it in a bag or in anything besides on my feet."

"I would ask how you are doing," John said as he gave Chuck one of those looks only friends can give. "But I can see you're not feeling well."

"That's an understatement," I said with a weak smile. "I had pneumonia once and I still don't remember feeling this bad."

"Robert said something about you being cursed by a warlock," John said as he looked at me with a raised eyebrow. "How do you know you were cursed and not just really sick?"

"Why don't you gentlemen have a seat," Selene said before I could reply, as she sat on the arm of the couch and put her arm around me.

"I know I was cursed because he told me so," I replied as the four men took a seat. "Not to mention, I went from healthy to terminally ill in three days. Overnight, I went from red spots on my stomach to red and black blotches. I'm no doctor, but that sounds a little rapid for even the most severe cancer cases."

"I've heard of this curse," Scott said and everyone looked at him. "It's called the Helicobacter pylori curse. A friend of someone I knew was cursed with it. The effects are very aggressive. The victim didn't even last a week. We never found out who put the curse on him. I don't think there's a cure for it, but we did find a tonic that will slow down the effects and give you a little relief."

"That's better than nothing," I said and even though it wasn't a cure, at least I'll be able to function.

"I heard rumors that if you kill the warlock who cursed you, the curse will be removed," Selene said and the idea of killing Brian did appeal to me.

"That's just a rumor," Chuck said and my hopes were dashed again. "Then again, you can always make the warlock take the curse off you by threatening to kill him."

Robert, John, and Brian just looked at Chuck and he said, "What? It's just a thought. I mean, even if you're bluffing, he doesn't know that."

Chuck did have a good idea. All I had to do was find Brian, kill Antonio and his minions, and force the warlock to take the curse off me. It wasn't me who killed his daughter in the first place. Maybe, he'll listen to reason and take off the curse, and if he doesn't I'll just blow his brain out.

Selene looked at Scott and asked, "What do you need for the tonic?"

"It's actually a simple mixture," Scott replied as he got up and headed for the door. "I have everything I need in the car. I'll be back in a second."

After Scott went outside Robert looked at me and asked, "I know it's none of my business, but why did a warlock put a curse on you. We're not stupid, Jack. A couple months ago you asked for wolfsbane. I thought it was weird, but I didn't ask. Now a powerful warlock put a deadly curse on you. What are you and Selene involved in?"

"You wouldn't believe me, Robert," I

replied not know what to say to him.

"Actually, we would," John said and he had a serious look on his face. "We've see a lot of weird things in our lives."

"Werewolves?" I asked and John nodded "Well, now you know what the wolfsbane was for. As for the warlock, he was getting revenge for the death of his daughter."

Robert stared at me with big eyes and John looked at me with a judging stare. Chuck's expression never changed. He actually looked like he had a slight smile on his lips. I didn't like the way everyone was looking at me so I added, "I wasn't the one who killed her. I just happen to be in the wrong place at the wrong time. I even told the warlock I wasn't the one responsible for his daughter's death. To top it off, the person who did confessed to it, but the warlock is still holding me as one of the responsible people.

"Why don't you go to the police?" Robert asked and I guess he saw the flaw in his question right after he asked it. "Duh. Forget I said that. How could you possibly prove such a thing? You would probably end up in a padded cell before they believed you."

"Now you see my dilemma," I said as Scott

came back in with an old medical bag.

"Could you boil me some water, Selene?" Scott asked as he handed a little packet to her. "Once the water starts to boil, add these herbs to it."

I watched as Selene walked off into the kitchen, then Robert asked, "So, a werewolf? What was that all about?"

"That's actually a long story," I replied, not wanting to talk about it. "I'll tell you some other time."

Robert nodded and didn't pry for more details about the werewolves. I guess he noticed I didn't want to talk about it.

Everyone watched as Scott pulled out a silver goblet. It looked like something you could buy at a renaissance fair. Scott noticed everyone's face expressions when he took out the goblet and said, "All the components must be mixed together inside a silver container. The purities from the silver is one of the ingredients.

Scott added the components to the silver goblet, then he set it aside until Selene came out with the herbal water she boiled. She handed the tea kettle to Scott and he poured it into the goblet with the rest of the ingredients. He let the mixture absorb together, then once it was cool enough to drink, he handed it to me and said, "Drink it all."

The mixture smelled horrible and tasted even worse. As the tonic went down my throat, it went numb. I felt the potion travel through my system until it reached my stomach. Once it did, the pain completely stopped and I felt my strength begin to return. I sat up on the couch and couldn't hide my smile. I actually felt great.

"Well, I can tell by the look on your face, my tonic worked," Scott said as he gathered his stuff together and put it back in the medical bag. "I know you're feeling great right now, but in about ten minutes you're going to crash. The tonic was loaded with antihistamines, enough to knock you out until tomorrow morning. So, if I was you, I would head straight to bed before you pass out on the floor."

"You're not kidding," I said as I stood up and stumbled in the process. "I'm already starting to feel woozy."

"You better get him to bed," Robert said to Selene as he stood from his seat. "We can see ourselves out."

Selene reached over and took me by the arm.

It was a good thing she did, because I was about to fall over. My eyes were drooping and my speech was starting to slur as I said, "Thaks evrywon."

"You can thank us later when you're more coherent," Robert said as he and the others headed for the door. "You need to find a cure for that curse and if you need my help, just ask. I don't want to lose any more friends."

With those words everyone left and Selene helped me to bed. I had just enough time to change into my sleeping attire and lay down. Once my head hit the pillow, I knew nothing more.

Chapter Eleven

I woke later in the night to a disturbing and alarming sight. Before I even opened my eyes, I knew something was wrong. I felt supernatural and it wasn't coming from Selene. I opened my eyes, and sure enough, Zombie Show was staring down at me. He stood two feet away, not moving. Once Alan noticed my eyes were open, he took a step forward and his hand shot out towards me. I quickly threw off my covers. With reflexes I didn't know I had, I lunged from where I was, over Selene, calling her name in the process.

The were-panther woke as I landed on the floor next to her. She was instantly aware of everything in the room. Selene transformed into her hybrid form and stood between me and Zombie Shoe.

The zombie didn't come any closer. It just stood there, staring at me. Then a gurgling sound came from its throat and when the zombie opened its mouth, I could have sworn I heard it say, "Hhhooollllaaaddaaayyy."

At first Selene and I just looked at each

other, then Zombie Shoe said it again, but more clearly this time. "Hhoollaaddaayy."

"Shoe?" I asked, wondering if a part of Alan was in there. The zombie walked to the edge of the bed and stopped. It just looked at me with no emotion. "Alan, are you in there?"

Zombie Shoe walked to the foot of the bed, and this time he unmistakably said my name, "Holladay."

I took a step towards Alan, but Selene stopped me. "Don't go any closer to it. This may be a trap."

I stopped and as soon as I did, Zombie Shoe took two long strides towards me. Alan still didn't show any emotion, but Selene pushed the zombie back as she yelled, "RUN! Get out of here, Jack!"

For some reason I didn't want to run. Zombie Shoe didn't seem as threatening as before, so I hesitated. That little bit of time gave the zombie the advantage it needed to recover. This time it shambled, quickly, towards us.

Never taking her eyes of Zombie Shoe, Selene yelled at me, "What are you doing?! Get out of here!"

I was slow to react, but I stepped onto the bed and stumbled off the other side. Zombie Shoe turned to follow me, but Selene kicked the back of its legs, making the zombie fall to the ground.

While the zombie was getting back on its feet, Selene grabbed her cell phone and followed me out the door. Together, we ran down the stairs and out the front door. Like before, we got in her car and backed out of the driveway, as Zombie Shoe slammed against the front door. The door broke from its hinges, falling outwards, and Alan with it. As we drove off, I saw Zombie Shoe get to its feet and start to follow us.

As she drove, Selene called Xylon on her cell phone. While she did I fetched our spare change of clothes from the back seat. Selene suggested we keep some back there just in case this happened again. I thought it was a good idea, and so happens, it was.

Once Xylon answered the call I heard Selene say, "Xylon, it happened again."

"No, Jack doesn't need more stitches," Selene replied to whatever Xylon said. Even with the situation were in, I saw her crack a smile. I didn't think it was funny. "Were going to stay at a motel tonight, but were going to need some money until tomorrow."

"Alright," Selene said after a short pause. "We'll be right there. Thanks again, Xylon."

With those words Selene hung up. We drove to Xylon's house up on the North side of Pueblo. He lived on a short street named Peakview. It looked like a nice neighborhood. Xylon's house was next to a park. Actually, the park kind of surrounded his house on two sides. It looked like a really nice place to raise kids.

As we pulled up to Xylon's house he came out to meet us. I noticed his house was the only one with lights on. Then again, at three-o-clock in the morning, who else would be up?

Selene rolled down her window as Xylon walked over to the car. He handed Selene some money and then asked, "Are you guys sure you're alright?"

"Yeah," Selene replied and I could hear the irritation in her voice. "We have to put some kind of protection spell on the house to stop Brian from teleporting the zombie in."

"I don't know who were going to find to do that," Xylon said and the only people who came to mind was John and company.

"I'll talk to Robert tomorrow morning," I said and Xylon just looked questionably at me. "Maybe John knows someone who can cast spells."

"Who's John?" Xylon asked as he looked back and forth between me and Selene.

"They're the Wicca's Robert knows," Selene said as she quickly switched into her change of clothes. "Earlier, they helped Jack with his curse. They couldn't cure him, just ease the pain."

Xylon agreed that talking to John was probably our best bet. Once Selene was finished getting dressed he went back inside to get some sleep. Cleo stayed at La Luna to keep an eye on Zeana and Shaun so Xylon could have a break. Selene felt bad about waking him up in the middle of the night, but we had no choice. All of our money and credit cards were at home

First thing in the morning we're going have to get another door installed on the house. I called Jean Luke and asked if he could secure the house for us until morning and if possible, find Zombie Shoe and put him back in his grave. He agreed, then hung up.

Once we got to the motel Selene got us a room. They thought it was weird we didn't have any luggage, but Selene explained to the clerk that our house was being exterminated. He bought it and we headed up to our room.

I took a quick shower since I didn't have one earlier, then I climbed into bed. Selene was already there, waiting for me. Once I turned off the light Selene curled her body against mine, nuzzling her head under my chin. I put my arm around her and within a few moments, we were fast asleep.

Chapter Twelve

I called Robert the next morning, but no one answered. Besides finding a way to keep Zombie Shoe out of our house, I also wanted to find out if they heard anything about a cure for my curse.

I took a shower and got dressed. It was nice not having to vomit blood this morning, and my stomach hardly hurt at all.

Selene wanted to go to La Luna so she could give Xylon a break and check in on Zeana. I wanted to see how Shaun was doing, so I figured on my way to La Luna I would stop by Robert's and see if he's there.

Once I was ready to go I kissed Selene goodbye and went out to my car. Robert lived on the opposite side of town from us. If you hit the highway it took about twenty minutes to get there.

Once I was there I saw Robert's car parked outside his house. I got out of my car and walked up to his porch. The first thing I realized was the door is ajar. I pushed it open and said, "Robert, are you home?"

There wasn't any response so I stepped inside. As soon as I did I saw Robert's wife, lying on the floor to the right of the door. I walked over to her and saw she had her throat ripped out and was lying in a puddle of her own blood.

I left the house and went back to my car. As soon as I opened the door I heard a phone ringing. On the driver seat I saw a cell, which I knew wasn't Selene's or mine. I answered the phone and heard Antonio's voice on the other end say, "Hello, Jack. How do you like the present we left you?"

"You're a sick piece of crap," I replied and I couldn't wait to meet this vampire again. I had a wood bullet with his name on it. "Where's Robert?"

"With us," Antonio replied and I could tell he was enjoying this. "If you want to see him alive, meet us tonight and bring Katrina and Shaun."

"Where?" I asked and I was already tired of his game.

"Enterprise road, out by the airport," Antonio replied and I knew where it was. There's a warehouse out there with no name on it and a chain link fence going all the way around. Meet us there at dark or you will see Robert again, but not as you remember him."

There was a moment of silence, then another voice came on the line, "Hey, Jack. This is David. Why don't you head over to Aces pizza? I left you a little gift."

After those words I heard sinister laughter over the line, then there was a click, and it went dead. I could only fear what David meant. It was still early in the morning and Aces didn't open for a couple hours.

I called Tom right away and was happy when he answered. I told him about what happened to Robert and also what David said. Once Tom heard that he said, "I'm on my way."

I started my car and for the first time since I bought it, I burned rubber. Luckily, Robert only lived five minutes from Aces, so I arrived a good twenty minutes before Tom. From the outside everything looked normal, except for the fact the store didn't open for two hours, but all the lights were on. I wanted to go inside and have a look, but I figured it was best to wait for Tom. I didn't want to go inside anyway. I really didn't want to see the horror David had waiting for us.

Chapter Thirteen

Once Tom arrived I got out of my car to meet him. I saw the worried look on his face as he walked over to me.

"I take it you have yet to go inside," Tom said and I shook my head. "I wonder if we should call the police before we go inside. I personally don't want to see what's in there."

"If we call the police first, then we would have to explain how we knew about the crime scene before we even entered," I said, and Tom saw the logic, even though he didn't want to go inside.

We stared at each other for a moment, then Tom said, "We can't just stand here. We have to find out what happened, if anything at all."

Tom started to walk towards Aces and I followed. The thought of all of this just being a vampire ruse was a nice fantasy, but we both knew when it came to vampires, it was most likely a tragedy.

As we got to the building, we both peered through the windows, but we couldn't see pat the counter. Tom opened the door and we walked in.

Tom froze instantly. I looked at him and he said, "I can already smell the blood."

I couldn't at first, but being a werewolf, Tom's senses were much keener than mine. It wasn't until I got around the counter, then I smelt the coppery scent of blood. Along with the smell came the visual. Bodies were everywhere, torn to shreds. People I have worked with for years, all of them, dead. Massacred, for no other reason than to teach me a lesson.

Tears filled Tom's eyes, and I became sick to my stomach, even with the tonic in my system. I couldn't stand the sight or smell of so much blood and I couldn't figure out how Tom did. I was about to leave, when I saw movement on the other side of the store.

Doing my best not to step in any blood, I made my way over to where I saw someone move. When I got there I saw Danny with multiple wounds. He looked in really bad shape, and it didn't look like he was going to make it.

Lying next to Danny was Frank's mutilated corpse. His limbs were torn off and from the horrific look on his face, I would say he was still alive when it happen. He either died from the shock or from loss of blood shortly after. No matter what the case, I was sure it was extremely painful. From the way it looked, Danny was forced to watch as they tore Frank limb from limb.

Danny looked up at me as I grabbed my phone to call La Luna. I needed Xylon here immediately, because being a vampyr, Danny couldn't go to a regular hospital. I started to dial the number, then Danny closed his eyes and stop breathing. I was too late. He lost way to much blood. I tried CPR, but there was no response. I didn't want to lose another friend. I've lost so many already.

With nothing more I could do I stood up from Danny's body and looked around for Tom. I saw him in the office with his elbows on the desk and his head in his hands. His body was trembling and I knew he was crying. Tears were also in my eyes, but lately I have cried so much, I don't know if there's anything in me to let out. In less than a week I may be joining my friends anyway. I seriously doubt Brian will lift the curse from me, even when his life is threatened.

"We need to end this tonight," I said to Tom as I walked over to him. "Before Antonio decides to go after our family members."

"Didn't Thomas tell you?" Tom asked as he looked at me with red, puffy eyes. "Since he's the new Alpha of the werewolves he's had them watching our family's houses. If any vampires came within a block of them, his pack would hunt them down and rip them apart."

"I haven't heard about any of this," I replied, not liking the idea of a werewolf being anywhere near my family, present company excepted. "I'll have to talk to Thomas a little later. We'll need his help anyways against Antonio."

"Count me in," Tom said as he stood from his chair. "They stepped over the line. If it wasn't personal before, it is now. They have killed my friends, ruined my business, and destroyed my life. Listen, talking to the police may take a while. You take off and gather forces. When all of this is taken care of, I'll meet you later at La Luna. Every one of those bloodsuckers are going to pay."

Chapter Fourteen

I left Aces Pizza and something told me it was for the last time. On my way over to La Luna I called Thomas. A couple rings later he answered.

Thomas stood about six feet tall and had neatly trimmed, short black hair, which was parted down the middle. He had dark brown eyes and looked to be in his late thirties. Thomas always wears an expensive looking suit and tie. I guess for someone who has been alive as long as him, moneys no option.

Thomas is one of the original few werewolves left who was created by The Druids of the Inner Circle. He was one of the first of their kind, back then they called themselves "Lupine." They were created to be protectors of the Earth and for centuries, that is what they did.

"Hello, Jack," Thomas said after he answered the phone. I was about to ask how he knew it was me, but then I felt like an idiot as I remembered, caller ID. "What can I do for you, my friend?"

I told Thomas about Robert and his wife, then I told him what Tom and I found at Aces. There was quiet on his end for a couple moments, then he said, "That makes sense they would go after your friends, since they couldn't get to your family. Once I learned the Vampire Council was in town I split my pack up between your and Tom's families. There hasn't been any attempts of Tom's side, but one vampire went after your mom and a small group tried to slaughter you sister and brother in law. Don't worry, they never even got close to your families houses."

I didn't know what to say, so I thanked Thomas. If it wasn't for him and the werewolves, my family would have paid the price instead. The only problem is, it made me feel worse about the deaths at Aces. They were killed because the vampires couldn't get to my family, which makes me blood guilty for every one of them.

Thomas must have sensed my feelings, because he asked, "Are you alright, Jack?"

I didn't want to talk anymore about Aces, so I told him about my curse. Now it was Thomas' turn to be quiet again, then after a couple moments he said, "We'll make this warlock remove his curse from you, one way or another. I'll bring some of my Pack with me tonight, but I'll make sure to leave some with your family, just in case this is a set up."

I agreed with Thomas. When it came to vampires, you couldn't be too careful. I just wished we didn't need to spare any of our forces; I knew we were going to need them.

I made plans with Thomas to meet us at La Luna a little before dark. I knew Katrina and her coven wouldn't be able to venture out before then. Now all I had to do was find the bloodsucker and persuade her to help us.

In the past I never wanted to know where Katrina was. The farthest she was away from me, the better. Now, though, I needed her. We shared a bond since the night she made me her human servant. I've been fighting with that bond ever since. Now, I was going to use that bond to find her, and once I did, I would be able to put the second part of my plan in motion.

Once I arrived at La Luna I parked my car in the back where there are less distractions, then I shut my eyes and concentrated on Katrina. I used our bond when I did and I immediately felt her presence. I followed it until I located where she was, and I was surprised when I found out. She was no more than a few blocks away from me, under the burnt ruins of the Crimson Chateau.

I remember that's where Katrina's old coven used to rest. It looks like the fire department never found the secret room where Katrina hid their coffins.

Many of her minions were killed during our battle with Nathaniel. I guess when she moved her coven to the mansion, they left the excess coffins behind. I guess in a way it was a good thing for her.

Once I knew where Katrina was I broke my concentration. It was a good thing she's asleep or she would know I was looking for her. Since she's none the wiser we can take her by surprise and force her to help us against Antonio.

Before I went into La Luna I called the mansion. I knew Jean Luke would be sleeping, but Jarvis was awake. The phone rang a few times before he answered.

"Hello, you have reached the Rousseau residence," Jarvis said and that was the first time I ever heard Jean Luke's last name. I immediately wondered if he was or was related to Jean-Jacques Rousseau, whose ideas influenced the French Revolution. "How may I be of assistance?"

"It's Jack, Jarvis," I said as I got out of my car. "I have a message I need Jean Luke to have immediately after he wakes up."

I told Jarvis everything which has happened and had him ask Jean Luke if he could meet us in the alley where the Crimson Chateau used to be. I told him Zack would know where the secret sewer entrance is.

This is it. Katrina's not going to be able to hide anymore. Its time she came out and faced the Vampire Council. By the end of this night, either they or we will be dead.

Chapter Fifteen

I went downstairs and saw Selene already had her Pride present. Zeana was feeling much better. Her spine had been mended, thanks to her regeneration ability. Cleo was sitting on the bed next to her, they were talking and laughing about something.

Xylon was checking the bandages on Shaun's leg. Considering what he went through, he looks a lot better. He had some crutches lying next to his bed, which meant he was getting up and around.

Selene saw me when I entered the room. She walked over and hugged me. I returned her hug, but she must have sensed something was bothering me because she asked, "What's wrong, Jack?"

I told everyone what happened to Robert and his wife. I also told them what Tom and I found at Aces. My eyes filled with tears when I mentioned Danny.

Everyone in the room was shocked and Selene hugged me again. She knew how close

Danny and I were. Out of everyone, Shaun seemed to be the most upset. He grabbed his crutches and hobbled off his bed. Shaun started for the stairs until I said, "What are you doing, Shaun?"

"I'm going home to get my guns," Shaun replied as he got to the stairs and wondered how he was going to hop up all fifteen without falling and breaking his neck. "After our fight with the werewolves I ordered something special from an old contact of mine. I was going to bring it to the graveyard a couple nights ago, but I figured my sniper rifle was better for that situation."

"You can't drive," Xylon said as he walked over to Shaun. "The only reason why you're even out of bed is because of the pain killers I gave you."

"Not only that, but your truck isn't outside," I said and Shaun stopped. "Someone's going to have to go for you, or at least drive you there."

"Let's go, Jack" Shaun said as he hopped up the first stair. Seeing he was determined to go no matter what, Xylon helped Shaun up the rest of the stairs.

I looked at Selene and she said, "You had better go with him. We don't want him shooting off his other foot. We'll be fine right here until you get back."

I kissed Selene, then followed Shaun and Xylon up the stairs. Once at the top Shaun pulled away and used the crutches as he hobbled to the front door. I grabbed the door for him and he went outside. He looked around for a second, then he asked, "Where the hell's your car?"

"It's in the back," I replied and Shaun just gave me one of those, if looks could kill, type of stares. "I'll go get it. Stay here."

I walked around to the back and got in my car. I drove around front and saw Shaun waiting for me. As soon as I pulled up he opened the door and put his crutches in the back seat, then hopped in.

Shaun moved shortly after I did. He now lives on Red Creak Springs Road, which is on the South side of town. As soon as you turn onto it from Pueblo Boulevard, it's a business district with a few four and eight apartment complexes. You go down about a half a mile and come to a street named Pennwood. That's where the upper middle class live. A couple miles down from them is a trailer complex, then about five miles out from there is Shaun's house. There's not much but prairie in between.

I asked Shaun why he lived way out here. He just said he liked his privacy and no one bugged him this far out. I don't even thing anyone knew there was a house way out here.

Once we were there I got out of my car and went around to help Shaun, but he refused it. With a little bit of a struggle he worked his way out of the car and grabbed his crutches.

Shaun's house was very secluded, with lots of trees surrounding it. His yard was nicely landscaped and the house looked immaculate. Not something you would imagine from someone who was a widower and liked his privacy. I laughed when I saw his truck parked in his driveway, Jarvis must have dropped it off.

We walked up to the porch and Shaun opened the front door. He led me to the kitchen. Besides the basic appliances and a microwave, the only other items in this room were a small table and two chairs. Under the table was a hidden hatch. I wouldn't have ever known it was there if Shaun didn't pull the table out of the way and lift it. The hatch was hidden in plain sight, kind of like the secret door in his last place.

"I moved all the good stuff down here," Shaun said as he hobbled down the first stair. I went to help him, but he waved me off. You can't always be here for me, Jack. I have to learn how to do this for myself. I refuse to be a crippled who does nothing, but sit around all day watching T.V. and reading the paper."

I followed Shaun to a big room. There were boxes lining the walls and a wide selection of firearms. I was sure the new toy Shaun was talking about was illegal, but with what we were going up against the extra firepower was appreciated.

There were other kinds of weapons as well. I saw a wooden sword, archery equipment, and a crossbow. Shaun called me over to a long wood crate. He handed me a crow bar and said, "I had a look inside after it came to make sure it was intact and ready to use."

"If it's already open, then why do I need the crowbar?" I asked as I lifted the lid.

"Because there's a small box in there that's still sealed," Shaun replied and when I looked inside, I was stunned. I reached in the crate to grab the contents, but Shaun stopped me. "I don't think so. You grab the box and open it."

I did as Shaun said and pulled the box out of the crate. With a little effort I opened it and sure enough there were bullets inside. I watched Shaun as he lifted the gun. I couldn't help, but be in awe.

One thing was for sure, I would never be able to shoot it. I could barely handle my shotgun, there was no way anyone would ever trust me with a freaking M60.

"I've been spending the last month making wood tips for all those rounds," Shaun said and I was still in jaw dropping awe just looking at the gun. "I still have around seven hours of daylight left. That should be plenty of time to switch out the tips. I also made some pipe bombs out of hollowed logs. We just have to make sure none of our bloodsuckers are in the area when we lite one of those bad boys. Grab that other box over there and let's hull this up to your car."

I did as Shaun said. It was slow going with him missing a foot, but we managed. Once everything was safely secured in the trunk of my car, we headed back to La Luna. Once we were there I had Xylon come out and help us downstairs with the crate. Needless to say, when he saw the M60 he had the same glossy eyed awe look I did. Guys and guns are pretty much like girls and diamonds, but you can't shoot a diamond.

The only thing left for us to do was prepare and wait. Shaun started replacing the tips of the bullets. He had me and Xylon help so we could get done faster. By the time we were finished, Thomas arrived with a group of six people. I sensed supernatural off them, so I figured they were all werewolves.

There was four men and two woman. One of the men had short, black hair, which was parted down the middle. He had brown eyes and wore black leather pants and a black shirt. He topped off his outfit with a black trench coat. Thomas introduced him as Jacob.

The second man was bald, but he had a black goatee. I couldn't tell what color his eyes were because he wore sunglasses. He wore a black shirt and blue Jeans. He also topped off his outfit with a black trench coat. Thomas said his name was Nick.

The third and fourth men were twins. Their names were Darrel and Earl. They looked and dressed exactly alike, shoulder length, brown hair and blue eyes. They both wore black shirts, with red ties, but instead of dress pants they wore blue jeans. The only difference between the two men was that Earl was missing a thumb on his right hand. If it wasn't for that I would never be able to tell the two apart.

As for the women, they both had long, black hair, but one was dark skinned. The fair skin woman's name was Tina, and the other was Jennifer. Tina wore a black mini skirt and a cut off shirt, which exposed her belly. Jennifer wore tight blue jeans, which looked like she was poured into them, and a red t-shirt.

Shaun loaded the bullets into his M60, put a strap on it and slung it over his back. Jacob looked at Shaun and said, "How do you plan on firing that thing. With one foot, the kickback on that thing would floor you."

"First of all," Shaun said as he looked coldly at the werewolf. "I have a stand for it. Second, it's none of your freaking business."

Jacob took a few steps towards Shaun, then Thomas stepped between them and said, "That's enough, Jacob."

"He started it," Jacob said as he stared menacing at Shaun.

"Actually, you did," I said and Jacob looked questionably at me. "You know. A little over a month ago when you and your furry buddies tried to kill us."

I heard a giggle come from one of the two females and saw it was Tina. I looked at her and asked, "I'm sorry, did I say something funny?"

"Yeah," Tina replied with a smile. "You

called us furry. That's the first time I've ever been called that. It's usually beast, mongrel, or other hurtful words. I like you, Jack. I'm happy we didn't kill you the last time we… well, kind of met."

"Well, he's spoken for," Selene said as she walked over and took my hand in hers. "So keep your beastly, mongrel paws off him or I'll show you a few nasty words you haven't heard."

I smiled at Tina, doing my best to hold in my laughter. She didn't seem at all angered by Selene's comments. All she did was smile and say, "I see why you chose her as your mate, Jack. I also know when I'm outmatched. This round goes to you, Selene."

Tina turned from us and started to talk to Jennifer, while Jacob did the same with the other werewolves. I couldn't hear what they were saying, but I was sure Selene could. I would have to remind myself later to ask her, if there was a later.

Thomas apologized for his Pack. I didn't hold it against him, he only been their Alpha for a little over a month. I'm sure it would take time for their complete obedience.

Once all the tension in the room was at a

minimum, Tom walked in the door. As soon as I saw him Thomas, Selene, and I walked over to him.

"Everyone, except for Robert was killed," Tom said and there were tears in his eyes. "The only reason why he survived was because the Vampire Council already has him."

I couldn't believe it. People I've worked with for years, all of them gone. This couldn't go unanswered for. The police would never figure out who was responsible for this slaughter, and if they did, what could they possibly do?

I looked at my watch and saw it would be completely dark in fifteen minutes. It was time to convince Katrina to help us. I just hope we don't have to kill too many of her minions to get it.

Chapter Sixteen

Just before dark we arrived at the burned down ruins of the Crimson Chateau. I had Xylon open the manhole cover in the alley. I guess I could have had anyone but Shaun do it, since were the only people without supernatural strength.

Once the cover was off I dropped down with Selene, Xylon, and Thomas. Shaun wanted to come along. He figured his M60 would be very intimidating. I agreed, it would have, but with his missing foot, it would have been hard for him to get in and out of the sewer. Not to mention, I liked the idea if Katrina refuses to help, she and her coven will try to escape out the manhole and come face to face with Shaun and his M60.

It was pitch dark inside and I couldn't see a thing. We walked down the long sewer drain, staying to the sides to avoid stepping in a little stream of water, which was flowing down the center of the tunnel. Personally, I don't know how I missed it when dropping in.

"Hey, Shaun," I said as I stared into the darkness. "Can you through me down a flashlight?"

A moment later I saw Shaun's hand appear through the opening with a hand sized flashlight. At first I didn't think it was big enough to make much light, but when I turned it on, I was amazed. Light filled the tunnel, and now I could see, I noticed we were in a metal pipe about four feet wide and seven feet high.

Xylon led us down the tunnel. We walked about thirty feet until I told him to stop, then I said, "When we were last here, this is where Tyrone opened a secret door in the wall."

Xylon pushed on the wall where I was pointing and it moved inwards. We moved through the opening and Xylon closed the door behind us. He looked at me and saw I was staring questionably at him, then he said," The closed door may slow them down a little if they try to escape."

I nodded and looked down the new opening. With Shaun's flashlight I saw we were in another tunnel, but this one slanted down. Xylon took the lead again and we followed. The tunnel continued onward at a slant until we came to a dead-end. I showed Xylon where to push on the wall again, and another door opened. We walked into a large room and the last time I was here I remembered it being lit by ceiling lights. I felt around on the wall for a switch, and once my fingers came across it, I flipped it and the lights burst to life. The room had a red carpet and dark oak paneling covered the walls. As I looked around the room I saw ten coffins. Nothing has changed since my last time here, except there were less coffins.

We had just a few moments before the sun was completely down, then Katrina and her coven would rise from their coffins. We really didn't have a plan. I figured it was better only a few of us came down here to talk, less threatening that way. We don't want to kill Katrina's coven, we want them to help us. Still, I don't have any problem with killing a couple of them if Katrina refuses to come peacefully.

As I was trying to think of some way to persuade Katrina to help us without bloodshed the lids on four of the coffins started to open. We watched as the four vampires sat up. Shocked, Katrina instantly looked at us and said, "Jack, what are you doing here? How did you find us?"

"I used our bond to find you," I replied and Katrina looked surprised. "I take it from your expression you didn't think I could figure out how to do that. As for why we're here, the Vampire Council wiped out Aces Pizza and took one of my friend's captive. If you, I, and Shaun don't show up immediately, they're going to kill him."

"So, let them kill him," Dallas said and I so wanted to shoot him. "He's not my homie."

"Shut up, Dallas," Katrina said as she noticed my hand inching towards my gun. "Let's keep this quick and simple, Jack. If I refuse to help you, what's the consequences?"

"We start killing your coven one at a time until you do," I replied and Katrina didn't show any emotion, but Dallas did.

"You're going to pay for those words," Dallas said as he took a couple steps towards me before Katrina stopped him.

Dallas looked at her and asked, "You're not going to take that from him, are you? He's disrespecting us."

"Dallas, you are new here and don't understand who we are facing," Katrina replied and Dallas looked at us for a moment, then back to her. "Selene is the Alpha of her Pride. Her power rivals my own. Xylon is her second in command and strong enough to become the new Alpha. Thomas is an ancient werewolf and more powerful than all of us combined. To top it off, I'm sure Jack has the rest of Selene's Pride and Thomas' Pack up top waiting for us."

"Not to mention Shaun, Jean Luke and his coven," I said and I was bluffing about Jean Luke's coven. I didn't know if they were outside or not. I hoped they were here by now, but you never know."

"Alright, Jack," Katrina said and she had the look of someone who had been beaten. I guess of late, she has lost much. "Let's get this over with. I'm going to have to face the Council sooner or later, anyway. I guess I was just hoping for an easy way out."

"I've learned over the last few months," I said with a sigh. "When it comes to the supernatural, there isn't an easy way. Everything always ends in bloodshed."

We left Katrina's sleeping chambers and walked back down the tunnel until we came to the manhole. I offered to give Selene a boost up, but she just laughed at me and leaped out of the sewer. I shook my head and looked around for a ladder. I didn't see one, but I didn't need it anyway. Xylon picked me up and boosted me through the opening. Selene grabbed my arms once I broke the surface and pulled me the rest of the way. I was starting to get jealous of their supernatural abilities.

As soon as I was out of the sewer I saw Jean

Luke and his coven waiting for us. I was happy to see the bluff I told Katrina turned out not to be one. Now the gang was all here, we were ready to make plans and set them in motion.

One by one, everyone else popped out of the sewer. As soon as Dallas saw Shaun standing there with his M60, he got a mixture look of surprise and awe on his face, then said, "No freaking way. Where did you get that bad boy?"

I knew Dallas was talking about the gun, but I wanted to say, "Shaun has been with me from the beginning of this nightmare," but I figured right now was a bad time for jokes.

"None of your freaking business," Shaun replied, much to Dallas' discouragement. "All you need to know is where the bullets are going to go if you come any closer."

"Hey, homie. You didn't need to bite my head off," Dallas said and I wondered if that was vampire humor. "Before I became a vampire I use to have a big collection of guns."

"Oh yeah," Shaun said and he actually looked a little intrigued. "What happen to all of them?"

"I didn't see any use for them anymore,"

Dallas replied as he stared thoughtfully at the M60. "Once I became a vampire I was more deadly than any gun. What's the sense in firing a bullet, when you're faster than one? Not to mention, where was I going to keep them? It's not as if our master's let us have a room to ourselves to keep our stuff in."

I thought about that for a minute. No private place to call your own. That must be a really sad existence, not to have any personal possessions. Your only purpose is to serve and protect the master. I was actually starting to feel sorry for the vampire underlings, well most of them anyway. Zack seems to be happy, but then again, he doesn't have a master. Jean Luke seemed to be fair. It made me start to wonder why Zack hasn't been adopted by Jean Luke, especially since the Vampire Council was in town. Weren't all rogue vampires slain if they didn't have a coven? Kiki sure seemed to believe so. She went as far as to make amends with me to become part of Jean Luke's coven. Something fishy is going on here. I just hope Zack isn't the smelly part.

My thoughts were interrupted by the ringing from the cell phone I found in my car. I answered it and heard Antonio's voice on the other end.

"Tick tock, tick tock," Antonio said with a mocking tone to his voice. "Time is running out for your friend. You have thirty minutes, Jack.

Then the main course starts without you."

There was a click then silence. I put the phone back in my pocket, looked at everyone and said, "That was our host. The party is about to start."

Chapter Seventeen

About twenty-five minutes later we were all standing outside the warehouse. All the windows were boarded up and besides a couple bay doors, there was only one other door that didn't have a chain and lock on it. I walked up to the door and pulled, it wasn't locked and opened right up. I shut the door again until everyone was ready to go in. Since we haven't made any plans, I suggested it was the first thing we did.

A few moments later a shadow passed over the moon. We all looked up and saw what looked like the outline of a horse flying through the air. Needless to say, my jaw dropped as I stared astonished at the creature. Everyone, except for Jean Luke and his coven prepared for a fight. As the creature touched down Shaun pulled out his shotgun and I did the same.

"Put yer weapons away," Jean Luke said as he walked towards the horse like creature. "She will not harm ya. Her name is Amalthea and she is ma servant."

"This is your human servant?" Katrina and I

asked at the same time. Jean Luke nodded and I took a couple steps towards it. I loved horses, but I have never seen one like this, or for fact, one who could fly.

Katrina glowered at Jean Luke and I could see the envy in her eyes. I don't know why. All Jean Luke had was a flying horse, she had me.

I put my shotgun away and Shaun did the same. Both of us approached the creature and once we were close enough I saw it wasn't a horse at all. It was shaped like a horse and had a long, white flowing mane like one, but its head looked like a dragon. Two white, winding horns grew out of its head, they looked to be around two feet long. At first I thought them to be part of the mane, but now I could see I was wrong. The creature's eyes didn't have pupils. They were solid silver and when I looked close enough I swore I could see small bolts of lightning emanating from them. The creature's body was covered with shiny, white scales and it had talons instead of hooves. It had a long tail, which looked like a lizards, but the end was covered with white hair. The tail had foot long spines protruding from the top of it.

I stared at the creature in disbelief, then I asked, "What is it?"

"She is a Kirin," Jean Luke replied and as he

did the creature began to take a different form. The Kirin's body reshaped itself until she was a young, beautiful woman with long, flowing, platinum blond hair and silvery blue eyes. She wore a white bustier, which looked like it was made out of scales. She generously showed a lot of cleavage and I tried not to look, but what could I say, I'm a guy. She wore what looked like a white bikini bottom, and thigh high leggings, which also looked like they were made out of white scales. Flowing from the back of her waist was a layered skirt, which went all the way to the ground. The skirt was made out of the same white scales as everything else. Around her waist was a long red sash, which dangled to her ankles. It also looked like it was made out of scales. In her left hand she carried a long wood staff, which was gold plated at the tip. Hovering in midair over the gold tip was a red gem. I've never seen such a thing, the again I've never seen a Kirin either.

"I've never seen her before," I said as I looked at Amalthea. "How long has she been your servant?"

"Since ah became a master," Jean Luke replied as he stroked Amalthea's long, platinum blond hair. "Ah met her te night ah left te mansion. It was her who gave me te power ta start ma own coven. Once te ritual tat bonded us together was complete, she had ta leave and settle affairs. Now she is back for good. Ah had her meet us here tonight."

Katrina stared at Amalthea, then to Jean Luke. I could see the hate and envy in her eyes, but she didn't say anything. I could see why she was jealous of Jean Luke. After all, her human servant was just a human, even though I was special. The problem with that is, I don't want anything to do with Katrina. I was forced to be her human servant, not willing like Amalthea was to Jean Luke.

Once everyone was finished gawking at Amalthea we started to discuss battle plans. While everyone was doing so I remembered to ask Zack about him being a rogue vampire. I looked at him and asked, "Has Jean Luke added you to his coven yet?"

"Nope," Zack replied with a smile. "And he's not going to."

"Won't the Vampire Council kill all rogue vampires?" I asked and Zack nodded. "Aren't you worried about them coming after you?"

"Not at all," Zack replied with a confident tone to his voice.

"Why?" I asked and before Zack could say

anything Jean Luke responded for him.

"Because Zack is powerful enough ta be a master of his own coven," Jean Luke said and everyone stared at him, then to Zack. "His power has grown greatly over te last couple months."

"Impossible," Kiki said as she looked dumbfounded at Zack. "There's no way Zack is as powerful as me."

"Your right," Zack said with a smile. "I'm stronger than you."

"How can this be?" Katrina asked and she took the words out of my mouth.

"Apparently, Katrina was holding Zack's true potential back," Jean Luke said and with every passing second Kiki was getting more and more furious. "Ah don't know if Jack had anyting ta do wit it wen he broke te bond between Zack and Katrina, but ever since ten his power has grown immensely."

"What did you do to him?" Kiki asked as she took a couple steps towards me, and this time it was my turn to look dumbfounded.

"I don't have the slightest idea what anyone's talking about," I replied as Selene stepped between us. Kiki instantly stopped her pursuit and stared at the were-panther. "I didn't do anything to Zack besides break Katrina's hold on him."

"Then how did he go from being one of my weakest minions to being more powerful than Kiki?" Katrina asked and Kiki shot her an icy glare.

"That remains to be seen," Kiki said and I caught a hint of annoyance in her voice.

"I don't know," I replied as I looked back and forth between both vampires. "Jean Luke mentioned that Katrina may have been holding him back. Maybe Zack has always been powerful, but he was never able to show his true potential. He's always been a great fighter."

"How can he be a master?" Kiki asked and she was on the verge of losing it. "He doesn't even have a human servant."

"Actually, in a way I do," Zack replied and everyone looked at him again. "She already committed to it . Jean Luke and I are completely positive the ritual will work, because we already share a bond. I just didn't want to go through with everything until tonight is over with. I didn't want her to get involved in this, even if it would increase my power."

Before anyone else could say anything, a scream came from inside the warehouse. I recognized it as Robert's voice. Before anyone could say anything I walked over to the door and opened it.

"Wait, Jack," Selene said as she followed me. "Don't go rushing in. It could be a trap."

"They're torturing Robert," I said as I looked at Selene. "It's been over thirty minutes. We need to go in now."

"Jack's right," Tom said as he joined me at the door. "Too many people I know have died today. I don't want to add Robert too that list."

"Ten let's do tis," Jean Luke said as he joined us. "Jack, you come in last wit Selene and Katrina. Shaun, do you tink ya can hide te M60 in yer duster? Ah don't want ta reveal it until ya have it set up."

"It will be awkward," Shaun replied as he opened his duster and did his best to conceal the gun. "If all of you stay in front of me until I'm ready, it may work. Though, if I was a vampire master I would like to know what the person lurking in the back is doing. Pulling this trick off would be a long shot. It might be better if one of you strong supernatural types use it, then we don't have to worry about setting it up."

"I'll do it," Dallas said and he sounded eager to use the M60.

"No," Jean Luke said and personally, I agreed with him. "Witout te M60 Shaun will be less efficient if we have ta fight. Also, not ta disrespect ya, Dallas, but ah don't know you. Ah prefer ta have someone ah can trust wit tat kind of firepower."

Even though Jean Luke tried not to, Dallas still looked offended. It looked like he was about to say something to the master vampire, but Robert screamed again. Without anybody saying another word, Jean Luke and Amalthea pushed past us and into the warehouse.

Next inside was Tom, followed by Zack, Tabitha, and Terrance. Kiki just watched Zack as he entered and for a moment she looked like she wasn't going to go in. She looked at me, then started for the door. She body checked me on the way in and Selene was about to return the favor, but I stopped her. I guess the truce was over.

Thomas and his Pack followed the vampires, and behind them was Tom. Katrina's coven followed him in as Shaun tried to blend in with the crowd.

The next to enter was Selene's Pride of were-panthers. Xylon led them in, followed by Tabitha, Terrance, and in the back was Cleo. She smiled at me as she walked by, and even though she didn't show it, I could tell she was scared. Cleo is the youngest person here, not even twenty-one. She became a were-panther because all her family was killed and Selene offered her a new one, not to mention all the were-panther abilities. Cleo accepted and has been part of the Pride ever since.

Last of all was Katrina, followed by Selene, then I brought up the rear. Just before I entered the warehouse I glanced to my right and standing no more than ten feet away was the little girl from the cemetery. At least I thought it was here. She just stood there, looking at me. I was about to say something to her, but Selene touched my arm and said, "Are you alright?"

"Yeah," I said as I looked at Selene. "I've seen that little girl before."

"What little girl?" Selene asked and when I looked back to where I saw her, she was gone. I looked around, but she was nowhere to be seen.

"I guess I was mistaking," I replied as I took

one final look around. "Let's go, we better get in there."

Chapter Eighteen

Selene and I joined the others and as I walked through the warehouse I saw vampire's everywhere. We stopped in the exact center of the building, and all the vampires gathered around. Sitting in front of us, on a make shift stage was the members of the Vampire Council.

Sitting on the far left was a blond hair, blue eyed male. His hair was short and parted to the side. He wore a black sweater and black dress pants. His facial expression was completely neutral. Katrina told me his name was Timothy.

Standing behind Timothy was a beautiful woman with long blond hair. She had big green eyes, larger than any I have ever seen. She wore a long green dress, which sparkled like when the sun shines on the leaves of a cottonwood tree. The more I looked at the dress, I swore it was made out of leaves, masterly sewn together. Katrina said her name was Tatiana, the queen of the fairies and also Timothy's human servant, or so to speak. At first I didn't believe Katrina. Then Tatiana moved just right and the light caught her wings. I couldn't see them at first, they were transparent.

Sitting to the right of Timothy was a woman. She was beautiful, even more so than Selene. Her porcelain skin was flawless, almost to the point where it made her expressionless face look like a pulchritudinous mask. She had long, flowing black hair and piercing blue eyes. She wore a form fitting, violet colored, sleeveless dress that went down to her knees. She topped off her outfit with black heeled shoes. She was the only woman on the Vampire Council and her name was Lithia.

Standing behind Lithia was a man with long brown hair and electrical silver eyes. He wore a black vest and black dress pants. Under the vest was a white shirt and dark blue tie. On his hands he wore black leather gloves. He topped off his outfit with a stylish, black trench coat, which went down to his knees. He almost didn't look human to me and Katrina confirmed he wasn't. She said he was actually a dragon in human form, a disguise he likes to use while representing his master. His name is Cadmus.

Sitting next to Lithia was a dark skinned man with short, wavy black hair. He had brown eyes and when he stared at me, it felt like he was looking through me. He wore a multiple colored, striped kufi, which covered most of his hair. He wore a grand bubu, which matched the color of his kufi. When I first saw him he reminded me as an

African tribal leader. He had a stern expression on his face. It almost looked like he was judging us. Katrina said his name is Gumede.

Standing behind Gumede was a stern faced man with shoulder length black hair that hung down over his glowing red eyes. He wore a black dress shirt and pants, with a red tie. He topped of his outfit with a black leather trench coat, which went down to his ankles. If it wasn't for his red glowing eyes I would have thought him as a human, but Katrina assured me he was far from. His name is Mazzikim, and he's a Djinn. I wasn't sure what a Djinn was, so Katrina explained to me it was a creature which exists on dimensions beyond the visible universe of humans. They can be summoned and at that time they will take on human forms. Once I heard that I wondered how a vampire could get a creature like that as a servant.

Sitting next to Gumede in a humongous chair was a mammoth of a man. Just staring at him made me sick. He had to be close to a thousand pounds. His hair was receding so he kept it cut extremely short. He had blue eyes, but they were so sunken back in his face, you could barely make out the color. His face was round with huge cheeks and several folds under his chin. He wore an Armani suit which had to be custom made to fit his obese body. Katrina said his name was Bruce and I shouldn't let his weight fool me. Even though he is dangerously over weight, he still has the speed, strength, and endurance of a vampire.

Bruce held a chain in his right hand, which led to a collar that was around the neck of a beautiful woman. Like all the other vampire servants, she stood behind her master. She had long black hair and red eyes. She was scantily dressed, wearing long lacey gloves, a black bustier, and string bikini bottom. She topped off her outfit with thigh high boots and a hair band made out of roses. Katrina told me her name was Ophidia. I was also not to look into her eyes or listen to her voice, for she was a succubus. Even I knew what they were. A supernatural entity who takes on the form of a human female in order to seduce men. Charming them until they are in a trance like stage, then the succubus feeds by slowly draining the man's life-force.

Sitting to the right of Bruce was Antonio. The vampire stared menacingly at me. I guess he's still upset about our encounter the other night. Standing behind Antonio was Brian. The warlock had an eye patch over his left eye. I guess one of the wood chips from my shotgun shell took it out. Brian stared at me, then he searched our numbers and I was sure he was looking for Shaun.

Standing in front of his master at the bottom of the stage was David. Chained to the stage next to the vampire was Zombie Shoe and Robert, at least it looked like him. His eyes were white and glossed over, and when he saw us he snarled and snapped his jaws. His jugular was ripped out and bits and pieces of his flesh was missing. Zombie Shoe had blood on his face, which made me believe the damage done to Robert's body was his doing.

The vampire eyed all of us, one at a time until he stopped on Zack. The two vampires exchanged blows in our last encounter and I was sure David wanted a rematch. The vampire saw the confused look on my face. I could have sworn I heard Robert screaming before we entered, then I noticed some sort of jeweled urn in David's hands. The vampire smiled at me, then he lift the lid on the urn. The screaming sound of Robert's voice bellowed from it. I figured it must have been some kind of magical item created by Brian. We were suckered into a trap. Robert must have been dead for a while, because he has already risen as a zombie.

"Katrina De Luce and Jack Holladay, step forward to be recognized," Antonio said as he glared down at us.

Katrina did as Antonio said, so I followed her and Selene followed me. We took about four steps in front of everyone else and stopped. I didn't like being called out by Antonio, and I really didn't like being put on the stand in front of the Vampire Council. Every one of them could destroy me with a thought, which kind of disturbed me. It's a good thing I went to the bathroom before I came, or I would be standing in a puddle right now.

"Why does the were-panther approach when she was not called forward?" Lithia asked and even though her face didn't show any emotion, her voice sounded intrigued.

"Her name is Selene," Antonio replied with a quick glance to Lithia. "She is the Alpha of the were-panthers and also Jack's mate."

"I did not know were-panther's picked mates outside their Pride," Lithia said as she looked down at us. "Does Jack plan on becoming a were-panther once the two of you are bonded?"

"Jack hasn't expressed any interest in becoming a were-panther," Selene replied and I heard a slight tone of remorse in her voice.

"So, you will relinquish your lead as Alpha to a human?" Lithia asked and I could tell she also heard the tone in Selene's voice "Even though he is going to grow old and die?"

"I love Jack," Selene replied and a tear

rolled down her cheek. "He has proven to me and my Pride to be a man of honor and morals. He would give his life for any of us and we would do the same for him."

"Is this true?" Lithia asked as she looked at the other were-panthers.

Xylon stepped forward and replied, "Yes, it is. He has proven to have every quality an Alpha of the were-panthers should have."

Lithia and Timothy looked at each other, then she said, "Selene may approach if she pleases, but her fate will be the same as Jack's."

If the Council choses to put Katrina to death, I would die as well. I didn't want Selene to share in my fate. I looked at her and was about protest, but she put her fingers over my mouth and said, "If you even think about going through this without me, you will go without sex for a whole month. Also, you will also sleep on the couch the entire time."

"You can see who is going to wear the Alpha pants in that relationship," Timothy said with a smile and even though it looked like she tried not to, Lithia laughed.

"I love it when a woman takes charge,"

Bruce said as he looked lustfully at Selene. "Well, in the bedroom anyway."

I wanted to storm up to that fat piece of lard and pop a whole clip into his mammoth belly, before finally putting one in his heart. I knew if I did it would start a war which none of us would survive from.

"Enough of this," Gumede said in a deep voice. "We are here to conduct the trial of Katrina and her human servant. Let's finish this so I can return to my own affairs."

"Then allow me to start," Antonio said as he stood from his seat and walked back and forth in front of the other masters. "I was contacted by Nathaniel a few months back. He told me Katrina was planning on attacking his coven and she was enlisting the help of Boris. The night of their meeting, Boris was killed by Jack."

"How did you find out about this if Nathaniel wasn't present?" Lithia asked as she stared at me with a disappointing, but yet respectful look.

"Sebastian, Katrina's old human servant told Nathaniel about her plans and what Jack did," Antonio replied and the members of the Council began to talk among each other. I couldn't hear what they were saying, but Selene could.

"What's going on?" I asked Selene.

"They're talking about you and Sebastian," Selene replied as she intently listened in on they're conversation. "Their wondering why Sebastian would betray Katrina and how you killed a master. Their also talking about the ability you have. The way you're able to control Katrina's power."

"How exactly does this ability work of yours, Jack?" Antonio asked and I shrugged my shoulders. "What do you mean you don't know?"

"That's just it," I replied as I looked at the Vampire Council. "I don't. All I know is I can feel Katrina's power. At first all I was able to do was magnify it, but now I can take it from her and use it as my own."

"It almost sounds like the servant has become the master," Lithia said and Katrina shot her an angry glance, which made the Council member smile.

"Can you show us how this ability of yours works?" Gumede asked and I couldn't believe my ears. Were they just giving us the opportunity to use our power against them? Far be it by me to turn down such an opportunity.

"Sure," I replied as I tried my best to hide my smile. "Anytime you're ready, Katrina."

Katrina released her power and I instantly sensed it. I felt as it began to flow over me, then I snatched it out of the air. I felt Katrina's power begin to build up inside of me. She was no longer in control, the power was now mine. I let it build until I reached my limit, and even though the stress was painful, I absorbed more. My head felt like it was about to explode and when I was sure I couldn't wait any longer, I released it.

I felt Katrina's power…no, my power, roving around the room. I felt every presence in the warehouse. I knew where every vampire was and how many, we were hopelessly outnumbered.

Once I pinpointed everyone in the warehouse, I sifted out our forces from theirs and caused pain. Vampires all around us, even David, fell to the ground and writher in pain. I looked up at the Vampire Council and their servants and saw their faces were full of strain. My power was affecting them, but not enough to end this. They were to powerful. The only servant it had effect on was Brian. I figured it was because he is human, not supernatural.

I felt each of the Vampire Council members

release their power and it forced mine back. Their power dwarfed mine and soon it was all around the warehouse. All the vampires quit screaming and got back to their feet. Antonio helped Brian up. Apparently, my attack affected him more than the vampires. I figured it was because he was human and didn't have supernatural strength and endurance.

"Very impressive, Jack," Lithia said and from that moment on she looked at me differently. "I see how you were able to kill two masters. Except for us Council members, you could have wiped out every vampire in this room."

"Such an ability is too powerful for a mortal to have," Gumede said and I could tell his feelings for me went from neutral to hatred, maybe even fear. "Especially, a mortal who hates our kind."

"I seriously doubt Jack hates all vampires," Timothy said as he glanced over at Gumede. "If he does, then why did so many show up to defend him. Personally, I think Jack is only against those who threaten him."

"Enough of this," Antonio said after helping Brian sit down. "We are not here to discuss Jack. We are here to put Katrina on trial. We all know she's guilty of treason against her kind. It doesn't matter if she killed Boris and Nathaniel or if Jack did. He is her human servant, whatever he does reflects on her."

"Then Katrina is innocent of all charges," I said and everyone looked at me. "Every vampire I ever killed was through self-defense. I was always attacked first, which means the vampires who attacked me is guilty of attacking a human servant. If I'm correct, that is unlawful by your laws and an act of war."

All the members of the Vampire Council looked at each other, then they began to discuss what I told them. From where I was standing it looked like Antonio was arguing against my case. After a few moments Bruce looked down at me and asked, "Can you prove this?"

"There has been witnesses to these accounts," I said as I looked at the mammoth of a vampire. "Jean Luke was a servant of Boris before his master was killed. Katrina brought him in, but he was too powerful for her to control, so he started his own coven. He saw the events that night."

"What say you, Jean Luke?" Gumede asked as everyone's attention switched to Jean Luke, which made me happy since it was no longer on me.

"Wat Jack says is true," Jean Luke said as he moved forward to present himself. "Boris attacked first. Jack was only defending himself."

I knew it wasn't completely true. I was defending myself, and Boris did attack first, but I wasn't Katrina's human servant at that time. I wasn't going to tell the Council that, and apparently neither was Jean Luke.

"Dragons can tell if someone is lying," Lithia said as she looked at Cadmus. "What do you say?"

"Jean Luke speaks the truth," Cadmus replied as he looked at his master. "Jack was defending himself."

"What about Nathaniel's son, Joseph?" Antonio asked and I could tell he was getting desperate. "Are you going to tell us he was also killed in self-defense?"

"Yes," I replied as I remembered the events from that night. "Joseph attacked a friend of mine. He was trying to lure me out so he could kill me, but I wasn't the one who killed Joseph. He had me and was about to finish me off, but my friend caught him by surprise and shot him."

"Who and where is this friend?" Bruce

asked as he looked at me with his beady blue eyes.

"Her name was Detective Sarah Oswald," I replied as tears formed in my eyes. "She was killed a little over a month ago by a pack of werewolves. You can ask Antonio if this is correct. He had his mole there."

"What he says about Detective Oswald being killed was true," Antonio said through clenched teeth. "But as for his story about her killing Joseph, I know nothing about."

Lithia looked back at Cadmus again and with a nod he said, "Jack speaks the truth."

"As for Nathaniel," I said as I looked at Kiki. "We have one of his ex-servants right here. She was present during our battle with Nathaniel. As a matter of fact, she fought against us. Nathaniel attacked Katrina in her home. Not only did he kill most of her coven, but many of the patrons who were present. He had Sarah, his human servant, burn the Crimson Chateau down. I arrived late with Xylon, Shaun, and Cleo. We knew we didn't have a chance with Sarah standing, so Shaun snipped her from across the room. I used my ability to subdue all the vampires in the room, except for Kiki, she ran. Once they were subdued, we killed them."

Once I mentioned Sarah's name I saw Brian tremble with rage. It's taking everything in his power not to attack us where we stand.

"Is this true?" Gumede asked with a slight sarcastic tone to his voice as he look at Kiki. I could tell after what I said he had a very low opinion of Kiki. He could join the club.

"Yes, it's true," Kiki replied as she stared at me with daggers in her eyes. "Nathaniel was sure Katrina was conspiring against him. He contacted Antonio, but there wasn't enough evidence, so he decided to take matters in his own hands. We attacked Katrina's coven."

Lithia looked back at Cadmus and the dragon nodded. The vampire stood from her seat and said, "Kiki speaks the truth. Katrina is innocent. I vote to adjourn this trial."

"Agreed," Timothy said as he also stood from his seat, then walked over to stand next to Lithia.

"Even though Katrina may have been conspiring against Nathaniel, she never went through with her plans," Gumede said as he also stood. "Katrina is resolved from all charges against her."

"Since the first three of us have voted for Katrina and majority rules, there is no sense in me saying anything," Bruce said and he didn't bother getting up.

Now it was Antonio's turn. Everyone looked at him and the pressure was on, even though his opinion didn't matter. After a few moments the vampire lowered his head and said, "Fine, so be it."

Everyone on my side started to cheer. We weren't going to be slaughtered after all. The only thing we had to worry about now was the curse Brian put on me. I looked at the warlock and he stared back at me. Even though they lost he still had a slight smile on his face. He knew I was still going to die.

"We are finished here," Lithia said as she started to walk off stage.

"Not quite," I said and Brian's smile wavered a little. "I wish to bring charges up against Antonio and his human servant."

Lithia stopped, then she and everyone else looked at me. Antonio glanced at Brian, then said, "This is absurd. Charges for what?"

"Your human servant directly attacked me,"

I replied and Brian stood from his seat as his face contorted with rage. "He placed a curse on me. Even as we speak, I am dying. David and your other minions also attacked me and Selene after they delivered your invitation to a meeting, which I declined."

"Are these accusations true?" Timothy asked as he looked at Brian and Antonio.

Brian said nothing. He just stared at me with death in his eyes. Antonio knew it was impossible to lie to the Vampire Council so he replied, "Yes, the accusations brought up against us is true. With everything Nathaniel told I believed Katrina to be guilty. Brian, my human servant, wanted revenge for the death of his daughter, Sarah. Since I figured Katrina was going to be destroyed after the trial, I let him cast the curse on Jack."

"Now you see you are wrong and Jack wasn't even the one who pulled the trigger," Lithia said as she looked at Brian. "The curse will be immediately removed and the two of you will be put on trial."

"Never," Brian said as he glanced back and forth between Lithia and me. "Jack and Shaun will die."

"Who is this Shaun?" Gumede asked as he

looked at the small army I brought with me.

"I am," Shaun said as everyone moved aside. Shaun was sitting on the ground with his M60 attached to a stand. He had the gun aimed at Antonio, then he smiled as he chambered a bullet. "I suggest you take the curse off Jack."

"I'll die first," Brian said as his hands burst into flames.

"Antonio," Lithia said as she took a couple steps towards the vampire. "Have your servant stand down and remove the curse from Jack, or you and your coven will pay the consequences with no trial."

Antonio looked at Brian, then to me. I don't know what exactly made him do it. Maybe he knew Brian wasn't going to lift the curse no matter what. Or maybe with all the evidence against him he already knew the outcome of the trial. But for whatever reason he shouted, "KILL THEM ALL!"

With those words Brian shot a ball of fire out of his hands at Lithia. Once the fireball hit her she instantly burst into flames. I could hear her scream over the roaring fire.

While Antonio's minions attacked, Brian began to cast another spell. A moment later a huge glowing doorway appeared on the ground in front of the stage, then one by one a dozen creatures burst through. Each of them stood around twenty feet tall, and wore nothing but a dirty old loincloth. They were extremely muscular and could pass for giant humans if it wasn't for their facial features. Every one of them had red beady eyes, but the part I found most disturbing, they had snouts and tusks like pigs. Each of them carried long wood spears as weapons, easier longer than two men combined and rounder than my leg.

"Trolls!" Jean Luke screamed as the creatures lumbered towards us. "Don't let tem grab ya."

Everybody ran in different directions as the trolls attacked. David released Zombie Shoe and Robert. The two zombies attacked the first vampire they saw.

I stayed with Katrina and Selene remained by my side. I heard Shaun's M60 going off. I knew with him missing a foot he was going to be slow. I looked over at him and saw a troll just a couple strides away. Shaun ignored his pending doom and kept firing at the monster. The bullets penetrated the creature's thick skin, every time one hit blood would splatter from the wound. By the time the troll reached Shaun, the creature had over a hundred bullet holes in it. The troll fell dead, its momentum carrying the creature forward. A moment before Shaun was squished under the creature's massive weight, Dallas sped in and scooped him up in his arms. Shaun was saved, but the M60 was flattened.

"I got you, homie," Dallas said as he carried Shaun to safety. He looked a little perturbed from being saved by a vampire, but it was better than the alternative.

Bruce and Gumede jumped off the stage while ordering thei r minions to fight the trolls and Antonio's vampires. Timothy stayed by Lithia's side as she screamed from the flames. There was nothing he could do.

Cadmus transformed into his dragon form. He looked like a thirty foot gold lizard with huge wings and a long neck. The dragon began to speak in a tongue I couldn't understand, then the flames covering Lithia extinguished. She was badly burned with parts of her dress was melted into her skin. She laid on the stage, not moving.

One of the trolls climbed up onto the stage and it creaked from the creature's massive weight. The troll took a stab at Timothy with its spear, but the vampire dodged it easily. Seeing her master was in danger Tatiana whispered a few words I couldn't hear and a moment later, branches ripped up through the floor. Within a few moments they soared up into the air, forming a thirty foot tree. The roots of the tree ripped from the ground and it took a step after step towards the troll until it was between the creature and Timothy.

The troll swung its spear at the tree, but it was deflected aside by the branches. Seeing an opportunity to strike, Cadmus took a deep breath and breathed fire on the troll. The creature's skin blistered and it howled from the pain. The troll hurled its spear at the serpent with tremendous might. The spear pierced the dragon in the shoulder and sunk deep. Cadmus roared from the pain, but before he could do anything the troll leaped onto him, both of them falling to the ground behind the stage.

While Cadmus fought the troll, Timothy knelt next to Lithia. He looked at Tatiana and asked, "Can you heal her?"

Tatiana whispered some more words, then a few moments later Lithia's body glowed and her wounds began to heal.

"She still needs time to rest," Tatiana said and her voice sounded like the wind on a warm summer day. "She won't be able to defend herself if attacked."

"Then we shall give her the time she needs," Timothy said as he took a defensive stance over Lithia's body.

Cadmus and the troll rolled on the ground in mortal combat. The creature howled as the dragon bit down on its massive arm. Jerking his head from side to side, Cadmus severed the trolls arm. The creature rolled away from the dragon as it clenched its stump. Cadmus seized the opportunity and breathed on the troll again. The creature writhed in pain, but that only made the dragon intensify its attack. After a few agonizing moments the charred remains of the troll quit moving. Cadmus ceased his attacked, the troll was dead. With a roar of pain the dragon pulled the spear from his shoulder. Dropping the weapon he reverted back to his human form, then rejoined Lithia on the stage. Cadmus saw Timothy standing guard over his master and went to join him.

Zack saw a troll lumbering towards him, instead of getting out of the creatures way, he charged it. I could have sworn Zack was dead when I saw the troll stab at the vampire, but with super reflexes Zack dodged the spear, then he leaped onto the troll's arm and ran up it to the creature's shoulders. Zack wrapped his legs around the troll's neck and squeezed, while ripping out the creature's eyes with his claws. The troll howled in pain as it reached up to grab Zack. Seeing the creature's massive hands coming towards him, the vampire squeezed with all his might until there was a loud "snap." The troll's body went limp and crashed to the ground.

Zack hit the ground hard and tried to roll with the impact, but got the air knocked out of him. He laid there for a moment, completely stunned. Zack tried to get to his feet, but was unsuccessful. I saw Kiki walk over to Zack and hold out a hand to him. He accepted the help, but while she was pulling him to his feet, Kiki slammed his claws into Zack's gut. The vampire doubled over as he cried out in pain. I went for my gun as Kiki grabbed Zack by the hair and pulled his head back, revealing his jugular. I fired a moment before she struck. My bullet grazed her arm and Kiki jerked, but her claws still found their mark.

Kiki looked at me and smiled as I fired off two more shots at her. The vampire easily dodged both bullets, then disappeared into the commotion around us. I ran over to Zack with Selene by my side. I knelt down next to him and when he saw me he smiled. The side of his neck was ripped out and even though Kiki missed his jugular, she still ripped open an artery. Zack was bleeding to death. I looked down at him as tears filled my eyes and said, "Hold on, Zack. We're here to help you."

"It's alright, Jack," Zack said as he coughed up blood. "Kiki got me real good. Make sure you get her for me."

Zack coughed up more blood and went into convulsions as his body hemorrhage the life giving fluid. Tears rolled down my cheek s as I looked at Selene. A moment later Xylon was by our side. I looked up at him and he said, "Heal him, Jack. Use the strength of our Pride like you did when we fought the werewolves."

I felt Selene's power flow from her body as she opened herself to me. A moment later Xylon's power intertwined with Selene's. I absorbed their powers into my body, much like I did earlier with Katrina's. I forced the energy into Zack and this time instead of pain, I used it to heal. The wounds in Zack's neck and stomach began to mend. I felt his life force coming back. Zack's eyes fluttered open, then in a weak voice he said, "Behind you."

I looked up right in time to see David taking a swing at my head. Xylon was instantly between us, and if it wasn't for the were-panther David would have decapitated me. Xylon deflected the vampire's blow, then retaliated with a kick of his own. David crumbled over, the air knocked out of him. See the vampire was vulnerable, I aimed my gun at him and pulled the trigger. The bullet struck David in the chest, sending him staggering back a few feet. He fell to the ground in a heap of ash, then his body imploded into the little black marble.

Xylon reached down and picked up Zack. He looked at me and said, "I'll get him to safety. You two better get back to Katrina."

As we hurried back to Katrina, another troll burst through the ranks. It stormed towards Selene and me. When the creature was within twenty feet of us, Cleo and Zeana attacked it. After shifting into their hybrid forms, the were-panthers tried to slow the troll down by ripping at its legs with their claws. The creature ignored the minimal damage and continued its attack. Selene transformed into her hybrid form a moment before I saw something rocket over our heads. The object hit the troll in the head and It exploded. The creature crashed to the ground in front of us. I looked in the direction the projectile came from and saw Jarvis standing by the entrance with a bazooka in his hands.

Amalthea transformed into her Kirin form as Jean Luke leaped onto her back. Amalthea took to the air and flew over a troll. Jean Luke jumped from the Kirin to the back of the lumbering creature. The vampire sunk his claws deep into the trolls back, then began to climb. The troll screamed and tried to grab Jean Luke, but it couldn't reach the vampire.

Tabitha and Terrance watched their master rip into the troll's back. Since he had the creature's attention, they decided to take out its legs.

While the troll had its concentration on Jean Luke, Tabitha sliced the tendon on one ankle while Terrance did the same to the other. Not able to support its weight and longer, the troll fell. As soon as the creature hit the ground, Jean Luke ran the rest of the way up to the troll's shoulders. The vampire then reached around the creature's thick neck and ripped out its jugular.

Another troll came up behind Terrance and Tabitha. Neither vampire noticed it, but Jean Luke did. He yelled a warning to his minions, but it was too late. The troll stabbed Terrance in the back, skewering him like a shish kabob. He was dead before he hit the ground. His body turned to ash, then imploded into the little black marble.

Next, the troll turned its attention to Jean Luke. Seeing her master was in danger, Amalthea landed and transformed into her human form. Once the transformation was complete, she said a couple words I didn't understand. Amalthea's staff began to glow an eerie white color, then she slammed the butt end of the staff on the ground. Immediately, lightning struck down through the roof, sending debris everywhere. The bolt hit the troll in the head and the creature's body went into spasms from the current which ran through it. Both of the troll's eyes exploded and its head was completely charred. The creature fell, stone cold dead, to the ground with a loud thud.

Thomas and the rest of his Pack transformed into their werewolf forms. I saw Tom do the same, then all seven werewolves attacked a troll. With teeth and claws they ripped at the creature's legs. The troll reached down to grab one of the werewolves, but they were too agile for the clumsy oaf.

Seeing one of its fellow brutes having problems, another troll threw it spear at a werewolf. The weapon skewered the werewolf to the ground. Knowing you needed silver or magic to kill a werewolf, I figured it hurt like heck, but it would survive. At least, until the troll reached down and grabbed the werewolf. With both hands it ripped the lycanthrope in two. At that moment I really hoped it wasn't Tom.

The two halves of the werewolf started to revert back to its human form. I remembered Thomas telling me a while back, supernatural creatures were also considered as magical. I would definitely consider a troll as supernatural.

As the second troll lumbered forward to join the fight, Ophidia came out of the surrounding

commotion and stood in front of the brute. The troll looked down and saw the succubus. It raised a foot to step on her and she giggled. The troll looked confused for a moment, then it shook its head. Ophidia smiled at the creature, then said in an innocent voice, "You really don't want to hurt me, do you big guy?"

The troll looked confused again and a blank expression appeared on its face. Ophidia giggled again, then Bruce slammed all one thousand pounds of his weight into the back of the troll's legs. The force buckled the creature and it fell to its knees. Ophidia kept eye contact with the troll while talking smoothly and seductively to it. The troll didn't move or even blink as Bruce gored his way into the creature's back. I don't think the troll knew it was dying as it fell face forward in a pool of its blood.

The second troll still battled the six remaining werewolves. I knew the big werewolf was Thomas, but I didn't know which one was Tom. The werewolf which was ripped apart wasn't him, it turned out to be Nick.

As his Pack kept the troll occupied, Thomas snuck around to the back of the creature. The troll's legs were already bloody stumps, then Thomas ripped out the creature's tendon. The troll fell and as it did it stabbed at Jennifer. The werewolf dodged the spear, as the creature landed right next to her. Seeing its pending doom, the troll grabbed at Jennifer. Being off balance from dodging the spear, the werewolf didn't notice the big meaty hand coming towards her. The troll's long fingers wrapped around Jennifer's slim body, then the creature squeezed. The werewolf howled in pain as bones began to snap. Thomas and the rest of his Pack ripped at the troll's hand in a desperate attempt to make the creature release Jennifer, but the troll squeezed harder.

Thomas picked up the troll's massive spear and stabbed the creature through the head, but it was a moment too late. There were several loud cracking noises, then Jennifer went limp in the troll's hand.

Once the troll released its grip. Jennifer's body fell forward as she reverted back to her human form. The troll was dead, but it came at a great cost.

Dallas and Shaun's stood back to back as they fought off vampires from Antonio's coven. Both of the other vampires in Katrina's coven was taken out right away, one by Zombie Robert, and the other by a couple of Antonio's bloodsuckers. I felt bad for never learning their names.

A troll saw them and figured a crippled and

a lonely vampire would be easy targets. The creature went in for the attack. Dallas saw the troll coming and warned Shaun, who at that time unloaded a whole clip into the creature. Unfortunately, his .45 didn't have the stopping power of the M60. The bullets which penetrated the troll's thick hide were only surface wounds and didn't stop the creature's attack.

The troll lifted its spear to throw, but before the creature could release, a glowing circle appeared on the ground under it. A moment later, a wall of flames shot up from the circle. The troll dropped the spear and screamed as its flesh melted away. Once the flames died down, the charred remains of the troll laid on the ground and standing next to it was Gumede and Mazzikim. The eyes of the vampire's servant glowed and red hot flames danced inside of them.

Seeing there was only a couple trolls left, Brian cast another spell. Another portal opened and this time, huge winged creatures flew out. There was so many of them I couldn't even count. The creatures started attacking everyone in the room who wasn't part of Antonio's coven.

We were horribly outnumbered and there was no way for us to win, not when Brian can port in creature after creature. I figured the only chance we had was if Katrina and I worked together.

Before my ability didn't work against the Council, but that was against all of them. I had to try again, and hopefully against Antonio alone, it would work.

I was just about to tell Katrina my plan when I sensed supernatural right behind me. I looked and saw Zombie Robert about to take a chunk out of my shoulder. I quickly shoved it away as Selene transformed into her hybrid form. Katrina was about to rip into Robert, but Zombie Shoe shambled up behind us. Katrina turned to face the new threat as she said, "You have to shoot it in the head. Taking out the brain is the only thing which will stop it."

With a powerful kick, Selene knocked Zombie Robert to the ground. The were-panther then pinned it to the ground with her supernatural strength. The zombie snapped at her as I hurried over and put the barrel of my gun to his forehead. I didn't want to shoot Robert, but I knew this was no longer him. I looked at him and said, "I'm sorry," then I pulled the trigger. The zombie's body jerked, then laid still.

As Katrina struggled with Zombie Shoe I walked over and shot him in the head. The creature just looked at me, then said in a guttural voice, "Holladay."

Zombie Shoe forgot about Katrina and came after me. I looked at Katrina and asked, "I shot it in the head. Why is it still trying to eat me?"

"This zombie was raised with a curse," Katrina replied as she grabbed Zombie Shoe and tossed it away from me. "It can only be stopped if the body is completely destroyed."

"How the heck do we do that?" I asked as I watched the zombie regain its footing and shamble towards me again.

"We need to burn it," Selene replied as she grabbed the zombie. Hurry, you and Katrina get things under control before those flying creatures notice us. I'll handle the zombie."

Like before, Katrina activated her power and as soon as I sensed it, I seized control. I let the power build up inside of me, then released it. Within moments I sensed everything in the warehouse. I hunted for Kiki, but she was nowhere to be found. I concentrated on the last few trolls and all the flying creatures. Once I sorted them out from everyone else, I located Brian and Antonio. I didn't bother with the vampires since I wasn't sure which ones were Antonio's.

Now I had all the enemy targeted, I caused pain. All the creatures and Brian fell to the ground, writhing in pain. Antonio, on the other hand, was only affected for a few moments. The vampire recovered quickly as he fought against me. He was much more powerful than Katrina, no matter how hard I tried to keep control over Brian and the creatures, Antonio pushed me out. Within a few moments the vampire completely dominated us. I felt Antonio's power fall upon me like a ton of bricks. It forced me and Katrina to the ground, then we got a taste of our own medicine. We screamed as Antonio's power wracked our bones. The vampire was in my head and I could hear him laughing. My head was splitting and I couldn't concentrate. I heard Katrina scream, or was I the one screaming. I was so disoriented I didn't know what was going on.

Darkness began to take me. I was sure I was dying, then things began to clear. I heard a faint voice in my head, but I couldn't make out who it was or what was being said. The pain started to subside and once more I was able to think. I heard the voice again, and this time I recognized it as Lithia's.

"I can only keep Antonio at bay for a moment," Lithia said as I felt like myself again. "You have a rare gift, Jack. Your bond with Katrina has nothing to do with it. Use it against Antonio. Absorb his power. Use it against him."

I did my best to do as Lithia said. Antonio was extremely powerful and I wasn't sure if I could keep control once I had it. I noticed Antonio was starting to use his power on everyone else, so I had to do something.

I didn't want to be consumed by Antonio's power, so I absorbed a little at a time. I became light headed and a little dizzy. The vampire's power was intoxicating. The more I let in, the more vigorous I felt.

As I absorbed Antonio's power I became less concerned about being consumed by it. I realized it wasn't much different than controlling Katrina's. At first there was more than my body could handle, but as I absorbed, my threshold grew.

Once I couldn't absorb any more, I pushed back. Antonio didn't expect to be attacked by his own power. I caught the vampire totally off guard. Slowly, I pushed his influence out of everyone and once the pain stopped they started to fight back against the creatures.

Antonio stared at me in disbelief. He tried desperately to regain control, but like Katrina's power, his was now mine to control. Antonio looked at Brian and yelled, "Do something! Stop Jack before he completely takes over!"

I saw Brian begin to cast a spell. I knew the warlock could still be a problem, so I had to do something before he finished. I focused on Antonio's power, then forced it towards Brian. I felt it rush towards the warlock like an invisible wave. The force-wave slammed into Brian, knocking him off his feet and disrupting the spell.

I felt Antonio try to regain control, but it was too late, his power was now mine. Once again I gained control over every creature in the warehouse and subdued them. Since I was using Antonio's power I was able to sift out his vampires from the rest. All of Antonio's minions began to scream as I induced pain unto them.

After Antonio's forces were subdued, I directed the power towards him. I saw the strain on the vampire's face as he tried to fight back, but it was in vain. I commanded Antonio to his knees, and try as he might, the vampire had no choice. Antonio dropped to his knees and I held him there. I watched as our forces slaughtered his, until he and Brian were all there was left. I noticed Selene, Zeana, and Cleo had Zombie Shoe subdued, so I looked at Katrina and said, "Bind Antonio and Brian."

Katrina was in a state of awe when she looked at me, but did as I said. Katrina had no problem finding something suitable to bind Brian, but knowing there were no bonds which could hold Antonio she grabbed one arm as Jean Luke seized the other.

Antonio glared at me and I ignored him as I walked over to Brian. The warlock looked at me and spit. The spittle hit me in the face. I was tempted to hit Brian, but I fought the urge as I wiped off the saliva. Once I was finished, I said, "Take off the curse."

"GO TO HELL!" Brian yelled and his face was full of rage. "You're going to die, Jack. Nothing can stop my curse."

I looked at Lithia and she confirmed it with a nod. Seeing I was going to get nowhere with Brian, I walked over to Antonio as I pulled out my gun. I pointed it at the vampire's heart and said, "Tell Brian to remove his curse or I will kill you."

"It doesn't matter," Antonio said as he looked at Brian, then back to me. "There's not a thing I can say to Brian to make him lift the curse. Were both dead anyway. If you don't kill us, the Council will.

I looked at Lithia and again she nodded. There was nothing I could do. I couldn't force Brian to take off the curse. I was going to die and there was no way to stop it. I stared into Antonio's eyes, and when he looked into mine, he saw death. Accepting my own fate, I pulled the trigger.

Antonio jerked as the bullet penetrated his heart. I saw the vampire's eyes gloss over as life left them. A moment later Antonio turned to ash and imploded into the black sphere. I heard a gasp from Brian as his heart also stopped. The warlock shared the same fate as his master. As Brian collapsed to the ground I saw him smile and with his final breath he gasped, "You lose, Jack."

Selene looked at me as she struggled with Zombie Shoe. I saw tears appear in her eyes. With the death of Brian, there was no cure for the curse. At most I had a day or two left. It was just enough time to say goodbye to family and friends.

As Selene struggled with Zombie Shoe I looked at Lithia and asked, "Is there a way for us to dispose of the zombie?"

"Yes, bring it here," Lithia replied as she gestured towards the stage.

Selene, Zeana, and Cleo rustled the zombie up onto the stage as Cadmus transformed into his dragon form. Once on stage Lithia instructed the were-panthers to release the zombie, then quickly get out of the way. They did as the vampire said, then when they were clear, Cadmus breathed fire on Zombie Shoe. The skin melted away from the creature's bones, and still the dragon continued. It wasn't until there was nothing but ash, then Cadmus stopped. Zombie Shoe was no more.

Selene came down off the stage and walked over to me. Tears streamed down her cheeks as she put her arms around me. I held Selene close, then a moment later Zeana and Cleo joined us. All the decisions I needed to make about me and Selene were made for us. With Brian's death, I needed worry about them anymore.

As I shared a moment of remorse with Selene and her Pride, everyone heard Katrina say, "Hold on one second. Jack killed Antonio."

Everyone looked at Katrina with confused expressions on their faces. The vampire sighed, then said, "My human servant just killed one of the Vampire Council members. That means there's an open seat on the Council, and since Jack was the one who opened it, the position belongs to me."

I was shocked to hear what Katrina said I didn't want to be her human servant, but even more, I didn't want to be part of the Vampire Council, not even for a day or two.

The four members of the Vampire Council

looked at each other, then they started to discuss the matter. After a few minutes Lithia looked at Katrina and said, "By our law, your statement is true. But as you know, Jack is cursed. In a couple days you won't have a human servant and you need one to hold a seat on the Council."

"A minor technicality," Katrina said and I felt like a toy which was no longer wanted. "Once Jack dies I'll get another servant."

"You piece of crap," Selene said as she took a few aggressive steps towards Katrina before I had Zeana and Cleo stop her. "If it wasn't for Jack you would have been killed by Boris. You would never have had this opportunity."

"Jack was nothing more than a pawn for me to use," Katrina said and I saw Selene struggle against Zeana and Cleo. "He served his purpose. Now I will find another servant, a powerful one. One that's obedient and submissive."

Selene struggled and struggled, but she couldn't break free. Katrina was right. I was her pawn and she used me like a master of the game would. I walked over to Selene and stood between her and Katrina. The were-panther looked at me and started to cry again. I cupped her chin in my hand and kissed her. Selene's muscles relaxed and for a moment she forgot about Katrina. I looked into Selene's eyes and said, "I love you."

I turned from the woman I loved and walked over to Katrina. The vampire watched me as I approached. I looked into her eyes, and said, "There's one things about pawns, Katrina."

"What's that?" Katrina said with a sarcastic tone in her voice.

"If played right, even a pawn can check mate a king," I replied as I pulled out my gun and shot Katrina in the heart.

Katrina's eyes went wide and Selene screamed. The pain I felt was like nothing I ever felt before. I saw Katrina turn to ash and implode into the little black sphere, then everything went black.

Chapter Nineteen

I opened my eyes and all I saw was light. It was so bright, I was forced to close them again. My chest didn't hurt anymore. As a matter of fact, I didn't feel anything at all. The last thing I remembered was shooting Katrina. Was I dead? Is this heaven? It didn't feel like I thought heaven would, or even look like it. I was expecting the feeling of peace and serenity, and also a bunch of angels flying around. Not a solid patch of light which was too bright for me to see.

A moment later things began to dim, so I tried to open my eyes again. This time I managed to do so. I looked around and saw I was lying on a solid white floor, which went as far as the eye could see on all ends. I looked up and it went on forever as well. This was totally weird. I was lying on a white floor, which went on forever. There were no walls and no ceiling I could see.

I got to my feet and looked around. I thought I had gone insane, but then I heard a voice behind me say, "Hello, Jack."

I turned and saw the little blond hair girl from the cemetery. She was smiling as she looked at me with her big blue eyes. For a moment I was speechless, then I asked, "Where am I? Am I dead?"

"You are nowhere, Jack," the little girl replied with a giggle. "And yes, you are dead. After all, you did shoot Katrina."

"Why am I here?" I asked as I looked around again, half expecting something to mysteriously appear.

"Your prayer is being answered," the little girl replied with a smile. "You wanted a cure for the curse and be released from the bond you shared with Katrina. Both of those are now taken care of."

"But I'm dead," I said and the little girl nodded. ""Where do I go now?"

"Home to your loved ones," the little girl replied as her body began to take on a new form. She grew to a little over six feet tall and became a being of pure light. Wings of light sprouted out of the being's back. To me it looked like an angel. The being of light smiled at me, then said, "It's not your time. Go home, Jack."

Once again, the light became too bright for me to see. I closed my eyes again , but I could still hear the voice as it said, "Go back… go back…

The light began to fade again and I still heard the voice, but it sounded different now. Over and over it said, "Come back. Come back to me, Jack."

I was confused, which one did it want? So I asked, "Make up your mind, do you want me to go back or come back?"

"Jack?" the voice said and it sounded a lot like Selene.

I opened my eyes and saw I was in the warehouse. Selene had my head propped up on her lap and everyone was staring down at me. The were-panther had tears streaming down her face as she stared at me with an astonished look on her face. I also noticed everyone else had the same stupefaction looks on their faces.

"Hi," I said with a weak tone to my voice. I smiled at Selene and she began to laugh and cry at the same time.

"Hi yourself," Selene said, then she hugged and kissed me. Everyone clapped or cheered. No one could believe I was alive. I couldn't even believe it myself.

Once Selene let me have a chance to breath,

I looked her in the eyes and asked, "Would you marry me?"

"Yes," Selene said and she started to cry again. "Oh God, yes."

Selene hugged me again, but this time she was joined by Zeana, Cleo, and Xylon. I keep forgetting were-panthers were huggers, but that's alright. I was in a hugging mood.

"Sweat," Zack said as he knelt down beside us. I was so happy to see him. I thought he was going to die, but except for being a little paler than normal, he looked great. "I'm going to through you one insane bachelor party."

Chapter Twenty

Selene and I agreed on a wedding day after we were sure there were no lasting effects from Brian's curse. We figured November twenty-first would be suitable. It gave everyone time to prepare and I was able to recuperate from my near death experience.

Over the last month Jean Luke became the newest member of the Vampire Council. He took over all of Antonio's assets and responsibilities. I couldn't think of anyone better to have the position, even though it meant we wouldn't see much of each other anymore.

Tabitha stayed with Jean Luke as his second in command. She let me know if I ever got tired of Selene, she would make herself available. I was flattered, but being with a vampire was too much like necrophilia.

Zack took over as the new master vampire of the city. It wasn't as bad as I feared. He took the role very seriously and he was actually a very good leader. There wasn't a single party at the mansion, well, except for my bachelor party.

Thomas continued as Alpha of the werewolves. Out of the Pack members he brought with him to the warehouse, only Jacob and Tina survived. Over the last month the werewolves turned out to be great allies.

Dallas joined Zack's coven after Katrina died. Over the last month he and Shaun spent a lot of time together. The two unlikely friends swapped stories and even went out to the firing range. I stayed in touch with Shaun, but with no supernatural creatures trying to kill us, we really didn't have much in common.

Jarvis returned to his role as butler of the mansion. I figured with Zack as the master of the mansion, Jarvis would want to retire by now. But the last time I saw him he looked as happy as he ever did, if you can call an emotionless mask as looking happy.

Tom shut down Aces Pizza. After what happened there he wasn't able to keep it going. He's gotten better control of his lycanthropy and has been spending more time with his family than Thomas. Tom started a new business as a carpet cleaner. He wanted me to work for him, but Selene said I was retired. She had plenty of money for us to live in the life of luxury for the rest of our lives.

Selene gave La Luna to Xylon. He spent all his free time there anyway. Zeana started to date Xylon and the two of them made a really cute couple. Cleo stayed working at La Luna. With how much she got paid, there was no place else in Pueblo she could make more. Selene was very generous to her employees, especially the ones who were considered family.

The Vampire Council members returned to their own affairs. Since I was the one who killed Antonio, I was offered an honorary position on the Council. I was going to decline, but after I thought about it, I figured it would be a good idea to have powerful allies. You never know when something supernatural will come lurking.

Selene flew my brother and his wife down from Wisconsin. They just had a baby girl and I was able to see my niece for the first time. I was excited about seeing my brother again after all these years, but there was someone else tonight I was really looking forward to seeing. I knew she would be here, especially after I spread the word around about Selene and me getting hitched.

The night of our wedding I was in my changing room, when there came a knock at the door. I opened it and saw Jean Luke standing there in a tuxedo. I've never seen his dressed up before and I would have laughed if he didn't look so good in it. He took time out from his Council affairs to be here tonight. He came all the way here for my wedding, but most of all we had unfinished business with my uninvited guest.

"She is here, mon ami," Jean Luke said with a sadistic smile. "I already have everyone in place."

"Thanks, Jean Luke," I said as I straightened my tie. "After tonight all the loose ends will be tied up and I can finally relax."

Jean Luke nodded, then he turned and walked down the hall. I shut the door and took a seat as I waited for my visitor. I didn't have to wait long, maybe five minutes before I heard the door open and sensed supernatural from behind. I stood from my seat and said, "I was wondering when you would show."

I turned and saw Kiki staring at me. She had a sadistically, evil smile on her face. Kiki giggled as she looked at me, then said, "You didn't think I would let you get married without me. I was actually hurt, Jack. After all we've been through together, you didn't even invite me to your wedding."

"I knew you would show anyway," I said as I steadied myself for an attack. "Or did you forget you were still one of Jean Luke's minions. He's kept tabs on you since the day you backstabbed Zack."

"Now it's payback time," Zack said as he walked into the room. Kiki turned and saw the vampire standing in the doorway. Beside him was Jean Luke and behind them was Tabitha.

Kiki looked back at me and said, "You piece of crap, Jack. You set me up."

"Duh," I said sarcastically. "I couldn't have you ruining Selene's special day."

There were no windows in this room, so Kiki had nowhere to go. Seeing she had no other choice, the vampire charged me. Being faster and stronger than Kiki, Zack and Jean Luke grabbed the vampire before she could even get halfway to me.

Zack had one arm and Jean Luke had the other. Kiki was completely subdued. As they held the vampire I pulled out my handgun. Then I reached in my pocket and took out a silencer, which was my wedding gift from Shaun. After installing the silencer on the gun I walked over to Kiki. The vampire pleaded to me. She asked for mercy, but after what she did, even if I wanted too, Zack would have finished her off.

I placed the barrel of my gun under Kiki's chin and pulled the trigger. The vampire's body turned to ash in Zack's and Jean Luke's hands, the she imploded into the black sphere. Zack bent over and picked up the marble, then he tossed it to me and said, "My wedding gift to you, Jack."

I smiled as I put what was left of Kiki in my pocket. Xylon appeared at the doorway and looked at me, then said, "Its time, Jack."

The five of us left the dressing room and entered the main hall. Jean Luke and Zack took their places as ushers and I joined my brother, who was my best man, at the altar. Xylon waited for Selene at the entrance. It was his job to give her away.

A couple moments later the wedding song started and as I looked down the aisle I saw Selene enter the room. She was dressed in an ivory strapless ball gown with veiled lacquer-print "Lily of the valley." All I know, it was elegant and very expensive, and Selene looked very beautiful in it. Zeana and Cleo were Selene's bridesmaids. Selene told me their dresses were Princess One Shoulder Knee Length Chiffon with Ruffle. I didn't know what any of that meant. All I knew was I was allowed to pick the color. Not knowing anything about bridesmaid's dresses I picked my favorite color, red. Selene liked it, so my job was complete.

Xylon was dressed in a tux. Now that I understood.

Once Selene met me at the altar, Xylon handed her hand to me. I took Selene's hand in mine as Judge Kinkel started the ceremony. I didn't remember much of it, I was too captivated by Selene's beauty. As I looked in her eyes, I knew she was the woman I wanted to spend the rest of my life with. By the time Judge Kinkel said, "You may kiss your bride," I was already in a stage of complete bliss. I pulled Selene close and kissed her gently. She returned my kiss passionately, and from that moment on I knew my life with Selene would be happy ever supernatural.

THE END